Butchered After Dark

Country Cottage Mystery #10

Addison Moore

and

Bellamy Bloom

Edited by Paige Maroney Smith
Cover by Lou Harper, Cover Affairs
Published by Hollis Thatcher Press, LTD.

Books by the Authors

Cozy Mysteries

Country Cottage Mysteries

Kittyzen's Arrest (Country Cottage Mysteries 1)

Dog Days of Murder (Country Cottage Mysteries 2)

Santa Claws Calamity (Country Cottage Mysteries 3)

Bow Wow Big House (Country Cottage Mysteries 4)

Murder Bites (Country Cottage Mysteries 5)

Felines and Fatalities (Country Cottage Mysteries 6)

A Killer Tail (Country Cottage Mysteries 7)

Cat Scratch Cleaver (Country Cottage Mysteries 8)

Just Buried (Country Cottage Mysteries 9)

Butchered After Bark (Country Cottage Mysteries 10)

Meow for Murder

An Awful Cat-titude (Meow for Murder #1)

A Dreadful Meow-ment (Meow for Murder 2)

Murder in the Mix

Cutie Pies and Deadly Lies (Murder in the Mix 1)

Bobbing for Bodies (Murder in the Mix 2)

Pumpkin Spice Sacrifice (Murder in the Mix 3)
Gingerbread and Deadly Dread (Murder in the Mix 4)
Seven-Layer Slayer (Murder in the Mix 5)
Red Velvet Vengeance (Murder in the Mix 6)
Bloodbaths and Banana Cake (Murder in the Mix 7)
New York Cheesecake Chaos (Murder in the Mix 8)
Lethal Lemon Bars (Murder in the Mix 9)
Macaron Massacre (Murder in the Mix 10)
Wedding Cake Carnage (Murder in the Mix 11)
Donut Disaster (Murder in the Mix 12)
Toxic Apple Turnovers (Murder in the Mix 13)
Killer Cupcakes (Murder in the Mix 14)
Pumpkin Pie Parting (Murder in the Mix 15)
Yule Log Eulogy (Murder in the Mix 16)
Pancake Panic (Murder in the Mix 17)
Sugar Cookie Slaughter (Murder in the Mix 18)
Devil's Food Cake Doom (Murder in the Mix 19)
Snickerdoodle Secrets (Murder in the Mix 20)
Strawberry Shortcake Sins (Murder in the Mix 21)
Cake Pop Casualties (Murder in the Mix 22)
Flag Cake Felonies (Murder in the Mix 23)
Peach Cobbler Confessions (Murder in the Mix 24)

"Do you ever get the feeling the inmates are running the asylum?" Jasper, my shiny new husband, muses as we both stare out the windshield at the grounds of the inn.

"Not funny," I say without taking my eyes off the malfeasance before us. "Although at present, a very real reality."

My name is Bizzy Baker, and I can read minds. Wait—let's do that again. My name is Bizzy Baker *Wilder*, and I can read minds. Not every mind, not every time—but it happens, and believe me when I say, it's not all it's cracked up to be. Like now for instance.

Why do I get the feeling someone's head is going to roll for this? Jasper groans as he looks out at the scene with his eyes set wide.

"Because you're right," I tell him.

Only a handful of people know about my strange quirk to pry into the human mind, and Jasper is one of them.

It's October, the scariest month of the year, and Jasper and I have no sooner arrived back at the Country Cottage Inn from our honeymoon than we're met with the biggest fright of them all. We just spent the last several hours driving from Vermont all the way back to our cottage nestled here in coastal Maine, only to find that the grounds of the inn I manage have been transformed into a virtual Halloween fantasyland. While we were away, I put the inn into the very capable hands of my best friend, Emmie Crosby, who assured me not a thing would go wrong. And now I'm beginning to question her definition of the word.

The inn itself is a stately two-story structure with blue cobblestones covered in ivy and an occupancy of over two hundred guests at any given time. It's set on vast acreages that also house over thirty cottages for nightly or long-term rental. Jasper and I happen to live in one—or we will now that we're officially married, my old cottage to be exact. It's just a short walk to the inn, but seeing the throngs of people here, it looks as if it would take me twenty minutes to do what I can normally achieve in three.

"Drop me off at the entrance," I say as I take in the carnival atmosphere with shock. It's evening, and there are enough twinkle lights strung up over every inch of the grounds to illuminate this place like a football field. There's a sign on my right that reads, *This way to the pumpkin patch by the cove!* "Pumpkin patch?" And to the left there's a huge wooden sign with the words *Welcome to the Cider Cove Fall-oween Festival!* "Fall-oween Festival?" And as we draw closer to the inn, there's yet a third sign that reads, *Purchase tickets to your worst frightmare inside at the front desk.* "Oh my goodness. What in the world is a frightmare?"

"I think we're living it."

I shoot a quick look to my newly minted husband.

Jasper Wilder is a tall, shockingly gorgeous, shockingly mine, homicide detective I met last year. It's safe to say things have gone exceptionally well for us—especially the last two weeks we spent holed up in the honeymoon suite at the Maple Meadows Lodge in Vermont.

A warm heat runs through me just thinking about our time there, and for the briefest of moments, I'm transported from this frightmare right back to our cozy little love shack. But we're not there anymore—as evidenced by the crowd of zombies that just stepped haphazardly in front of the car is quick to remind me.

"Hey, watch where you're going." One of the zombies slaps the hood of Jasper's nice ride.

"I believe *you* stepped out in front of *me*, buddy," Jasper says under his breath.

He pulls into the circle driveway right in front of the inn, and I swing the door open as the icy breeze envelops us.

A dull groan evicts from me. "Why do I feel like our magical honeymoon will officially be over as soon as I step foot outside of this car?" I lean over and steal a kiss from this caustically handsome man that fate somehow brought to my path. It's true, with his shock of black hair and pale gray eyes—have I mentioned the body built by the gods of Mount Olympus?—Jasper is sheer perfection both inside and out.

He pulls me in close. "How about we vow not to break the spell? I vote we unofficially continue with our honeymoon for the next fifty or sixty years."

"Sounds like a reasonable amount of time." I land another, far more lingering, kiss to his lips before hopping out of the car, and just then a thought hits me. "Ooh, I bet I'll get to see Fish and Sherlock first!"

Fish is my sweet black and white tabby, and Sherlock Bones is Jasper's red and white freckled mutt—but now he's mine, too.

"Give 'em a squeeze for me. I'll park and meet up with you."

Jasper takes off, and no sooner do I take a step toward the inn than a small black cat scampers in front of me. I've never been one to lean toward the superstitious side of things, but a chill rides up my spine, and a terrible feeling of foreboding hits me. If it wasn't apparent before, it's apparent now—a very dark cloud is sitting over the inn and I have the distinct feeling something wicked is about to rain down on us all.

"Hey, you," I whisper, bending over and snapping my fingers at the cute little kitty who looks like a stray. "Come here," I say. "Let me help you."

It turns my way and hisses with its yellow eyes glowing like high beams and I gasp at the seemingly supernatural sight. And then in a flash it disappears into the night.

The double door entry looms ahead with a colorful wreath comprised of fall leaves dotting each one. Last month, I had every square inch of the inn festooned for fall with colorful leaves and orange twinkle lights strung up along every counter and doorway. Pumpkins dot the entry, along with bales of hay, and there are a couple of scarecrows sitting on either side of the door. The oversized pots adorning our landscape are brimming with crimson and gold mums, and the maples that line the property have turned a fiery shade of red.

I hurry inside to find the inn toasty and decorated to the hilt for Halloween with witches' hats, ghosts, bats, and spider webs everywhere you look. The pumpkins that sat on the long marble counter have been replaced with glowing jack-o'-lanterns, and I see Emmie dressed as a zombie as she helps out a small crowd of guests who also share her sudden flair for tattered accouterments. In fact, everywhere I look, I see costumed guests.

The inn has gray rustic wood floors, dark mahogany wood paneling along the walls, and a grand staircase that leads up to the second level. And I can't help but note that fall leaves and orange string lights have been wrapped around the banisters that lead upstairs, and it looks like a fall wonderland in here.

Bizzy! My sweet cat, Fish, hops over and I quickly scoop her up and squeeze her tight while peppering her face with kisses.

I found Fish about two years ago as a stray outside of my sister's candle shop, Lather and Light. She's a cute long-haired black and white tabby—and yes, I can read the animal mind, too. Believe me when I say, on most occasions they have better things to say than humans.

Initially, Jasper and I wanted to take our pets, Fish and Sherlock Bones, along to Vermont with us, but Emmie talked us out of it. And since I once believed Emmie was of sound mind, Jasper and I listened.

Fish mewls as she nuzzles her face to my neck. *How I've missed you! And, of course, Sherlock has been a wreck without you. He's here, somewhere, milling around these monsters that have congregated at the inn. You have to do something. Emmie is out of control. She sold the inn to the Montgomerys and she's humiliating Sherlock by forcing him to dress like a clown. She tried to get me, too, Bizzy, but I hissed and ran for the hills. I wasn't above clawing at her, you know.*

"I'm going to run for the hills in a minute myself," I whisper into her tiny cold ear.

I'm about to make a beeline for my bestie when a man in a tan trench coat bumps into me.

He pulls back and nods. "My apologies." He's tall, built thick and stalky, handsome more or less, and about Jasper's age, mid-thirties to my late twenties. Has a dark, neatly trimmed beard and matching dark hair. His blue eyes siren out against his olive skin as he gives a quick glance to the left and right of me.

"Can I help you find something? My name is Bizzy Baker and I run the inn." I grimace because here, on the very first opportunity I had, I forgot to mention my brand new surname.

Bizzy Baker Wilder, Fish is quick to correct. *Don't tell me you've forgotten so soon. I didn't have that luxury. That nuisance Sherlock you left me with reminded me every single minute that I was a Wilder now like him.*

Normally, Fish and Sherlock get along, but I can see she's had enough of him at the moment.

"No. You can't help me," the man gruffs as he continues to scour the vicinity. *I'll find the little tart on my own, and then I'm going to kill her.*

He stalks off, and I freeze solid for a moment.

My word, I hope he wasn't being literal.

The crowd clears and I see not only Emmie Crosby, but I see Georgie Conner standing behind the reception desk as well. Georgie is sporting the zombie look right along with Emmie, and I'm sensing an undead theme there.

They both gasp in unison as they spot me, and before I know it, we're hugging it out and squealing right here in the foyer.

Both Emmie and I share the same dark shoulder-length hair and denim blue eyes. We share the same name, too, Elizabeth, but we've been going by our nicknames ever since we were kids just to keep our sanity afloat—not that it's been working for her as evidenced by the circus she's running.

"I can't believe you're back! Wait until you see the changes we've made around here." Georgie honks out a laugh as she pulls a giant porcelain doll from behind her back that looks to be about the size of a toddler. The doll is creepy with a bushel of red curls for hair, an eerie grimace, and wide amber eyes that stare vacantly ahead. Her cheeks are heavily pronounced, and she has a peachy glow, albeit she looks slightly covered with soot as does that dress of hers made of muslin and old lace. "Great news! I've got an entire haunted doll collection on display in the ballroom. And it'll only cost you six bucks to take a tour of them all."

"Haunted dolls? Wonderful," I say with all the enthusiasm one would bring to a root canal—at a haunted dentist's office no less.

Georgie Conner is somewhere in her eighties, has that whole Einstein hairstyle thing happening, lives in kaftans, and is the sweetest fun-loving hippy artist you'd ever want to meet. Her daughter, Juni, was married to my father for all of five minutes. Georgie lives here on the grounds, and I like to tease that I got her in the divorce.

She leans in. "So tell us! Are you knocked up? Can you walk straight?" She hoists her hand in front of my face. "How many fingers am I holding up?"

"All important questions," I say as I turn to Emmie. "But before I answer, I'd like to ask a few of my own."

Emmie winces. "I can explain everything. We had a freak electrical storm right after you left, and the Montgomerys' pumpkin patch suffered a huge fire. And you know they host the official Cider Cove haunted Halloween festival each year—and well, when they announced they were going to cancel it, I told them they could host it right here at the inn. I mean, we have the room. We have the meadow behind the cottages. That's where we have the midway with games, the food, the pumpkin carving, and the face painting, and the—oh, well, there's too much to mention. Of course, at night it's being transformed into a bona fide frightmare, which is strictly for teens and adults."

"Of course," I muse.

She lifts a finger. "Oh, and we decided to move the pumpkin patch to the sand, and the kids and the families are just loving it because they get to take a walk around the cove while picking out the perfect victim for their jack-o'-lanterns. The haunted hayride is just behind the meadow, and there's a haunted maze Jordy just finished constructing out in the back."

Jordy is the inn's handyman, Emmie's brother, and my ex-husband—it's a long story that involves Vegas, cheap liquor, and an Elvis impersonator. Suffice it to say, we were untangled from that matrimonial catastrophe quicker than you can say *I do not.*

Just as I'm about to say something, and God knows what that might be—I've got an entire river of words ready to erupt from my throat—a woman with caramel blonde hair and pale green eyes runs our way with the cutest brown and black Yorkshire Terrier in her arms.

"Emmie!" She waves as she struts over dressed in western gear with a denim shirt tied off under her bosom, exposing her midriff, and a pair of jeans that may or may not be painted on. She has an obvious beauty about her, slightly turned-up nose, bushy dark brows, and high cheekbones. She's a touch taller than me. I'm guessing same age range, and there's a polished confident look about her. "Is everything set for the block of tickets I purchased?"

"Oh yes," Emmie is quick to assure her. "In fact, all of the tickets have already been claimed. The frightmare began twenty minutes ago, so you should be able to find your friends as soon as you get out there."

Friends? She casts a quick glance toward the door. *I'm not sure I'd give them the honor.*

Emmie quickly hustles me over to the woman. "Blair, this is my best friend Bizzy that I was telling you about. The one who runs the inn."

The woman tips her head back. "The one on the honeymoon?" See lifts her hand in the air as she asks the question, and I spot a gorgeous silver ring on her finger with a golden rose. And in the middle of that rose a ruby gleams like a droplet of blood.

"That's right." Emmie winks my way. "Bizzy, this is Blair Bates. Blair, this is Bizzy Baker *Wilder*." Emmie gives a congratulatory laugh as she says it. "Blair is one of Camila's good friends."

"Oh." Any trace of a smile I had quickly dissipates from my face. And then, just like that, it rubber bands right back. As the manager of the inn, it's my duty to maintain a serene demeanor toward all guests—even those that are friends of my husband's ex-fiancée. Normally, I wouldn't mind that Jasper had an ex-fiancée, but this one just so happens to still have the hots for my husband. Camila has proven harder to get rid of than head lice. "It's nice to meet you, Blair. If I can help you in any way, please let me know. And who's your little friend?" I ask, giving the sweetie in her arms a quick scratch between her ears.

"This is my baby girl, Sprinkles," she says, dropping a kiss to her forehead.

Oh, so today I'm her baby girl? Sprinkles looks up at her owner. *I believe she called me a little devil this morning when I was gnawing on her shoe. It's not my fault it smells of top grain rawhide.*

A tiny laugh strums from me.

"Well, it's nice to meet you both," I say.

"Likewise." Blair glances to the counter. "And Emmie, your jack-o'-lantern hand pies are to die for." She dashes over to a platter brimming with miniature pies in the shape of jack-o'-lanterns and scoops one up. "And the pumpkin pie filling is magical. Have a great night, ladies," she says as she zips for the door. *As soon as Dr. Feel Good gets here, I know I will.*

Dr. Feel Good? I avert my eyes at the thought. And as much as I'd like to analyze that one, I don't have the time.

"Oh, Bizzy"—Emmie winces—"don't be mad."

"I'm not mad. I'm—bewildered."

Georgie rattles that haunted doll in my face and I jump.

"All right, Biz. Time for you to check out this circus." Georgie links her arm through mine. "Let's find Sherlock Bones. He's outside *paw*-trolling the grounds."

"I guess I should check things out. Technically, this is my circus, and like it or not, tonight these are my zombies."

"Are you ready, Bizzy?" Emmie takes me by the hand. "It's time for your biggest frightmare to begin."

No truer words were ever spoken.

Why do I get the feeling they're about to prove prophetic as well?

2

The month of October has always held a very special place in my heart. Not only is fall one of my favorite seasons, but Halloween ranks right up there with Christmas as far as holidays are concerned.

It's dark out, and the air is scented with cotton candy and sugary sweet churros, along with mulling spices from the hot apple cider. The sound of scary Halloween music blares from the speakers set out over the meadow, as we're treated to haunting organ music, only to be interrupted by the intermittent sounds of screams, a creaking doorway, and the ever intimidating ghostly howls.

Throngs of people clog the cobbled walkways as they struggle to get through the gates that lead into what from now on will be known as my biggest frightmare.

Lucky for me, Emmie leads us right up to the front where Jordy, my aforementioned short-lived ex-husband, lets us right into the nexus of the chaos.

"Hey, Bizzy!"

Jordy waves while surrounded by a group of girls dressed in skimpy costumes that show more skin than fabric. Jordy has on a furry hat of some sort and has fur lining his arms. I'm guessing he's a werewolf. Jordy has been known to be a playboy, and with his dark hair and blue eyes, it seems he's always swimming in a sea of estrogen. Let's just say, moon or no moon, he's no stranger to howling late into the night.

Jordy cinches an easy smile as he looks my way. "Enjoy the honeymoon? On second thought—don't answer that."

"Still wish I was there," I say as Emmie leads Georgie and me into what was once a peaceful meadow and has now fully transformed to resemble the inner circle of Hell.

Hay is strewn haphazardly all over the ground. There are mummies, zombies, and deranged looking men with chainsaws running around, traumatizing groups of teenage girls one at a time.

There are games set up with monsters at the helm, and a couple of trailers have been fashioned together in the back with the words *haunted house* blinking on and off in a neon sign above it. To the right there are a few carnival rides, a tilt-o-whirl, and the spinner, both of which I'm familiar with because I've been going to the Montgomerys' harvest festival since I was a kid. But I don't recall any ticketed event that promised to morph itself into my worst frightmare. Emmie explained on the way over it was a new ploy of the Montgomerys to churn out a couple thousand dollars a night, and judging by the thick crowds, they're getting more than that.

Georgie leans in. "Hold Annabeth while I find Juni." She thrusts the haunted doll into my arms and Fish squirms at the sight of her. "Boy, is Juni ever going to be glad to see you. We've been missing out on all the stakeouts and snooping your investigations bring on. But mostly we miss the dive bars and the strip clubs. How about we blow this monster mess and hit up a banana hammock cantina?"

"No," I flatline. "I don't anticipate a homicide in my future." Or a banana hammock cantina, but I keep the dream-killing commentary to myself. Instead, I shoot Emmie a look. "At least not a homicide I can't easily solve."

Georgie honks out a laugh. "That's my Bizzy. Not only does she have looks that kill, she knows how to get the job done, too. I'd watch your back if I were you, Emmie," she says as she takes off a like a bullet.

"Wait!" I call after her. "What about Annabelle?"

"*Annabeth*," Emmie corrects. "And you're not really going to kill me, are you?"

"Just a little. For fun," I smart as I rattle the terrifying doll in her face.

A sharp bark comes from my right. Before I can finish terrorizing my bestie, I spot a cute medium-sized pooch dressed as a clown, complete with a rainbow wig firmly attached to his head.

Bizzy Baker Wilder! Sherlock Bones barks like mad as he dashes my way, and I quickly bend over and give him some long overdue loving as he licks my cheeks, happy to see me—I'm guessing he's relieved, too. *The things Emmie has done to me. Would you please get me out of this contraption? I tried to tell her I didn't want to be the official Halloween dog of the inn, but she wouldn't listen. She's turned me into a canine version of a snowcone.*

Fish mewls. *Don't be a snow-cone-headed nitwit. Emmie can't understand you.*

"Hey," I whisper to Fish. "Play nice."

We have been playing, Bizzy! Sherlock jumps and leaps. *I've been playing with Emmie's dog Cinnamon and Leo's dog Gatsby. But Emmie keeps calling it roughhousing and tells us to knock it off.*

Fish yowls. *Because you're an oaf.*

"He is not an oaf." My chest trembles with a laugh. "And Cinnamon and Gatsby love you both." Cinnamon is Emmie's labradoodle, and Gatsby is Leo's golden retriever.

21

I'm not sure how, but the animals always seem to understand one another, and I'm glad about it, too. It's comforting to know they can communicate with one another.

"Hey, Bizzy," a deep voice strums from my right, and I stand to see Leo Granger, Jasper's best friend, smiling at me with that perennial mischievous look in his eyes.

Leo is a tall, dark-haired steed that's not hard to look at, and he happens to be in love with Emmie. Leo and I met last fall when we discovered we both share the same strange gift. We're both transmundane, and our ability to read minds falls under the category of something called telesensual. There are other powers that fall under the transmundane umbrella as well, but I don't know all that much about them.

But I wasn't always this way. Nope.

It wasn't until one of my supposed friends, Mackenzie Woods, dunked me into a whiskey barrel filled with water and apples at a Halloween party and I nearly died that I came to this strange condition.

As soon as that exercise in asphyxiation was over, four things happened to me. One, I have an irrational fear of bodies of water. Two, I'm terrified of confined spaces. Three, it initiated my general distrust of Mackenzie Woods—although it wasn't until she stole all of my high school boyfriends that I decided to part ways with her. Clearly, I'm a firm believer in giving people thirteen dozen chances. And four, I garnered the ability to read minds. Things have never been the same for me since.

Leo offers me a quick embrace. He and Jasper have been lifelong friends, with the exception of one interruption in which Leo made off with Jasper's then-fiancée, a wily woman by the name of Camila Ryder.

For the record, Leo nods my way, *Camila made off with me. She made the first move.*

Yeah, but you kept things moving, I tease.

Nevertheless, Jasper and Leo have moved right past it. In fact, Leo was the best man at our wedding, just like Emmie was my maid of honor. And seeing that they're in love, that made things extra special.

A pervasive thought that's been haunting my mind ever since my wedding day comes back to me, and my stomach knots up.

Right after the wedding, Leo let me know that he plans on filling Emmie in on his supernatural abilities. Leo says he's positive she's the one for him, and he doesn't want to keep anything from her as they progress. Which I agree with—the only caveat is, that puts me in a bind.

It's bad enough I've been keeping this secret from Emmie for the last thirteen years, but to continue keeping it from her after Leo divulges his truth, I don't think I could live with myself. So I plan on spilling my supernatural secret to Emmie, too.

I'm pretty sure she'll hate me when she finds out I've had the ability to pry into her thoughts all these years and never bothered to tell her. And that's exactly what I fear most.

She will not hate you, Leo says it curt with a quick nod as if to annunciate his point.

Emmie wraps her arm around my shoulders and squeezes me tightly.

"The four of us need to go on a double date asap." She tweaks her brows as her excitement over the prospect grows. "How's tomorrow night? I want to hear all about your honeymoon. Oh, and I want to see pictures. I looked the Maple Meadows Lodge up online and it looks amazing! I totally want to honeymoon there." She winks over at Leo and my eyes widen.

Have they been talking marriage?

I clear my throat. "I'm glad you saw the inn online because I don't think I took many pictures," I say. "We didn't really explore the grounds all that much."

Emmie bucks with a laugh. "You didn't leave the room, did you?"

Leo chuckles. "Sounds like a good time was had by all."

Sherlock barks. **Sounds like a waste of a good vacation. You could've slept at home, Bizzy. Emmie said they had hiking trails that led to rivers and** *endless meadows. I thought you and Jasper would be playing Frisbee a lot.*

They played other games, silly. Fish swipes her paw his way. *I bet Bizzy brought that ball of yarn we play with in bed. It's Bizzy's favorite thing to do before bedtime.*

We played in bed, all right, but there wasn't a ball of yarn in sight.

I cringe as I look to Leo, but before a smart-aleck remark could fly from his lips, the most frightening being of all pops before us—Camila Ryder herself, along with the blonde woman I met inside and that adorable fuzzy little Yorkie, Sprinkles.

"Well, if it isn't Dizzy Bizzy." Camila chortles as if it were the funniest thing in the world.

It's not all that funny or creative. Bullies and mean girls alike have been calling me Dizzy Bizzy for as long as I can remember. She'll have to try harder if she wants to impress me. But I know for a fact the only person she's looking to impress is Jasper. And that's exactly why she managed to score a position as the secretary to the homicide department a few months back. And don't think for a minute it doesn't irk me that she gets to sit in front of my husband's office eight hours a day. Well played, Camila. Well played.

Oh, wipe that sour look off your face, Bizzy. You look as if you're sucking on a sour piece of candy. Camilla winks as she says it.

Camila Ryder is a stunning woman with long chestnut brown hair that seems to have a life of its own. It dances down her shoulders in perfect perky waves, and her large dark eyes add that much more to her beauty. She has olive skin, perfect plucked brows, perfect bowtie lips, and I want to puke each time I see her perfect little self. She's dressed in a short blue frilly dress and is holding a staff taller than she is in her left hand. I'm assuming she's a slutty version of Bo Peep. More like a wolf in Peep's clothing—so basically, she's herself.

For reasons beyond my understanding, Leo shared his supernatural secret with her during the dark days when they were dating, and about a year ago she started to suspect I shared his strange gift, too. I've never come out and admitted it to her, but that hasn't stopped her from speaking to me telepathically either.

Camila clears her throat. "Bizzy, Leo, this is my good friend, Blair Bates. Blair, you've already met Emmie, the woman in charge. Bizzy is her underling and Leo is my ex."

Blair gives a gentle laugh. "Actually, Sprinkles and I met Bizzy a few minutes ago." She holds up that dark furry cutie in her arms. "This is some party. Thank you for the invite, Camila. And you're right, this will be the perfect venue."

"Venue?" I ask as I look from Camila to Blair. Normally, I would let the comment fly, but Camila is never up to any good, and the words *perfect venue* practically begged the question.

Camila nods. "Blair is a prominent realtor, and she's also somewhat of a socialite."

Blair shakes her head. "I'm no such thing." *I might be, but it's the wrong image, and I'm smart enough to know my image is everything at an event like this.* "I've simply invited a few of my good friends to join us this evening." She gives Camila a stern look, and not one of us misses the fact it was more or less a threat to keep her mouth shut.

Camila sniffs. "That's right. Just a little girls' night out with all the thrills and chills a scary month like this has to offer. We'll see you around."

They start to take off, and without hesitation, I block their path as I look to Blair.

"I'm sorry, I just wanted to let you know we have a full service pet daycare in the back of the inn called Critter Corner. And you're more than welcome to leave Sprinkles there any time you like. It's open every day of the week."

I try my best to scan her thoughts on why she might be needing a venue but come up empty. And sadly, I'm guessing that's the status quo with her—seeing that she's Camila's friend.

She smirks my way. "Thank you, but Sprinkles is fine with me tonight. She doesn't scare easily." Someone in the distance garners her attention, and a silent laugh bucks from her at the sight. *And lucky for me, neither do I.* "Excuse me."

She takes off, leaving Camila in her wake.

So much for being good friends.

Emmie's phone buzzes in her hand. "I need to get back to the front desk. I'm still on the clock, Bizzy. And don't you worry. I'm going to be working side by side with you all through the month. There is no way I'm saddling you with all of this. This is my doing, and I'm going to see it through to the end. Nothing will go wrong, I promise." She takes off just as a shard of lightning lights up the sky overhead.

"It seems someone upstairs begs to differ," I say, scowling over at Camila.

Be nice. Leo nods my way. "I'm going to see if I can help her out. Don't kill anyone while I'm gone." He motions to Camila with his head. *I'd hate to end the night with a homicide.*

I'm not entirely opposed to it, I tell him as he trots into the crowd.

I step in a touch closer to Camila. "What's really going on with your friend? Is she scouting this haunted venue for a wedding?"

She scoffs at the thought. "No, Bizzy. Only you have wedding bells on your brain." She makes a face at the doll in my hand. "It looks as if you and Jasper got right to work and made a lovechild. And she looks just as I suspected she would."

"Very funny," I say as Fish lets out a sharp yowl.

Please tell me that's not my sister. I don't think I can sleep on her head at night. She looks as if she eats kittens for breakfast.

"She's not mine," I say it more for Fish's benefit than for Camila's. Fish was so relieved I was back, she must not have noticed Georgie wielding the doll like the haunted amulet it is. "She's a part of Georgie's newly acquired haunted doll collection." I hold her out to the malfeasance in front of me. "Care for an early Christmas gift?"

"No, thank you." Camila shudders at the thought. *Now where did Blair go?* She cranes her neck past me.

"So how do you know this woman, Blair?" I get the feeling something funny is going on, and my feelings are rarely wrong. That's exactly why I've been able to solve so many homicide cases over the last year. Of course, Jasper isn't too thrilled about my involvement. But I say if a person stumbles upon a body, solving the crime becomes fair game to them—or *me* as my steady stream of bad luck would have it.

"I told you." Camila's voice grows snippy. "We're old friends."

Just past her, I spot Blair standing in a dark clearing way out where the meadow meets the woods. But she's not alone. There's a man with her, a tall man with a tan trench coat.

Hey? It's the man with the beard that I bumped into inside, and I grimace as his rather violent thoughts come back to me.

For Blair's sake, I'm hoping she's not the one he was looking to slaughter.

Not that I take what anyone thinks literally. I learned a long time ago to give people some serious leeway when it comes to their private musings. In all fairness, there are no rules as to what one can think of.

I watch as the man in the trench coat reaches forward and grabs Blair by the shoulders. For a minute, I think he's going to kiss her, but he gives her a stiff rattle instead and I gasp at the sight. He steps away before I can bolt over and knock him over the head with this haunted doll, and he reaches into his pocket and hands Blair what looks to be a thick wad of cash.

She carefully examines him before growing quickly animated. It's clear they're not having a happy exchange.

A crowd moves between us, and once it clears, both Blair and the man in the trench coat have disappeared.

A crisp, autumn breeze picks up and I shudder. But it's not the wind that has me chilled to the bone. It's that icy quasi-physical exchange.

Camila cranes her head past me and begins to wave wildly.

"Well, there you are!" Camila calls out as she waves a trio of girls this way. *How do you like that, Bizzy? I'm about to squash any and all theories of yours that insist I have no real friends.*

The trio of brunettes head over, and they all look pleasantly happy to see Camila.

Camila pulls them all in for a hug at once. "Bizzy, I'd like for you to meet my *friends*." She points to the brunette on the end dressed in a button-down blouse and long prairie skirt, with thick-rimmed glasses and a book in her hand. "That's Tabitha Carter—we used to waitress together way back when. She's still just a waitress, though."

The girl makes a face. *Leave it to Camila to dole out the backward compliments. Blair is seriously lucky I have a high pain tolerance when it comes to annoying people.*

"Nice to meet you, Bizzy." She pinches her button-down blouse and waves the book in her hand. "I'm supposed to be dressed as a librarian tonight. Everyone's been asking, so I thought I'd preempt the question." Her lips knot up. *Just a waitress?* She shoots Camila the stink eye. *Sometimes I wish Camila were a beetle so I could have the pleasure of squashing her.*

Me too, sister. Me too.

Camila laughs as if she heard the woman's inner ramblings. "And in the middle, we have Raven Marsh—who you can clearly see is an adorable vampire."

More like a vampy vampire, but I keep the commentary to myself. Raven is pretty with her long black hair that brushes up against her scantily clad bottom and big brown eyes with the longest lashes I've ever seen—and oddly enough, they don't look like falsies.

We exchange niceties as Camila points to the girl on the end who is wearing a tank top and short shorts. Both her arms and legs are covered with makeup that makes her limbs look as if she's morphing into a snake.

"And that's Sabrina Ames. Sabrina is a top-notch makeup artist as you can see."

"Wow," I muse as I inspect her work. "You've even got roses and tiny serpents and dragons drawn over your skin. You look amazing."

"She's a walking work of art," Camila gushes.

Sabrina has thick black hair that touches her shoulders and blunt cut bangs that fringe her icy gray eyes. She's pretty in an understated way and has an overall pensive look about her.

"Thank you both," she says.

Camila steps in. "Girls, this is Bizzy—the one who stole my Jasper away."

I can't help but avert my eyes at that one as I shed a quick laugh.

I'm about to correct her when Blair joins our circle. Her face is piqued, and the whites of her eyes are laced with crimson tracks as if she's been crying.

"Are you ladies all up to speed?" She sheds a forced laugh as she looks to her friends.

Tabitha glances to the sky. "Oh, don't you worry, Blair. We wouldn't dare get to the good part without you." Her expression hardens as she openly offers Blair a challenging look. "I think I'll go get a caramel apple before we begin." She takes off, and the mood grows somber in our little circle.

Raven laughs, exposing a set of pointed fangs in her mouth that go along with the rest of her vampire attire. She's got on a red bustier, with what look to be black swimsuit bottoms, fishnets, and a cape—and she might just get pneumonia out of the deal, too.

"Don't think about it, Blair." Raven winks her way. "I'll take care of Tabitha." *And then I'll take care of you.*

She takes off and both Sabrina and Camila exchange a cool glance.

I take it Blair is their fearless leader, and I'm sensing dissension in the ranks.

Fish mewls over at the shivering babe in Blair's arms. ***Don't worry, short stuff. Bizzy is my human, and she runs this place. She won't let anything happen to you. If you need anything, just bark. Bizzy can understand us because she's part animal.***

Part animal? I press my lips tightly to keep from laughing. Although, after the last two sultry weeks, Jasper might just agree with her.

Sprinkles lets out a sharp bark. ***Help! I'm in trouble. I see men with knives running around! I'm about to get butchered, I can feel it!***

Blair rocks the little cutie in her arms and sinks a kiss over her forehead to soothe her.

There are men with knives running around, but it's all a part of the haunted act—I hope.

Sabrina offers a stiff smile my way, and her serpent-like limbs seem to slither in this dim light. " So you run the inn with Emmie?"

"Sort of." It's actually the other way around, but no need to let my ego loose tonight. Judging by the screams, there are enough monsters among us. "Is there something I can help you with?"

"Oh no, I've already talked to Emmie. I'm doing a makeup tutorial with the guests as soon as I can fit it into my schedule. I guess she and her assistant Georgie have an entire slew of Halloween-themed activities lined up for the month. But I'm guessing the haunted doll collection is going to be the biggest hit." She takes a moment to snarl at the doll taking up residence in my left arm. "That's the creepiest thing I've ever laid eyes on, and I work in a dive bar."

A titter of laughter breaks out in our circle, and I'm slow to join in.

Blair nods to Sabrina. "We should get going. There's a lot we need to get done tonight." *Just because the word* **midnight** *is in our name, doesn't mean we need to start in the middle of the night. As soon as I can get this over with, I plan on hunting down that rat's hind end and teaching him a lesson.*

My mouth falls open. I bet that rat's hind end is the man in the trench coat. It's nice to see she's not letting him off so easily for shaking her like that. I hate to see any woman treated that way.

And what did she mean by they have the word *midnight* in their name?

Sabrina forces a smile, but it doesn't last long.

"All right, Blair, let's get this show on the road." *I've got a show of my own I'd like to put on—with you in private. There's no way I'm letting you get away with this.*

The three of them take off in a chatty flurry.

"Get away with what?" I whisper.

I don't know what you're talking about, Fish mewls. *But I smell trouble.*

Sherlock gives a few sharp barks. *Me too, Bizzy. And I'd much rather smell some bacon.*

The three of us take off, doing our best to find Jasper, Georgie, and Juni, but it's a three-way bust all the way around.

Down at the far end of the field, just past the rides and the bustle of bodies, I spot Blair and Tabitha, the woman dressed as a librarian, and judging by the way their limbs are gesticulating, Tabitha is about to knock Blair over the head with that book of hers.

I wander around for another twenty minutes straight, like a lost child right here at my own inn. I left my phone in my purse, which I left in the car, so I'm completely reliant on the old school method of tracking people down on foot. Come to find out, the old school method is nothing but an exhausting exercise in futility.

The music hikes up a notch, as do the screams of those unlucky enough to take part in this frightmare, and ironically, so does the headache I'm brewing.

I can't go ten steps without bumping into some costumed creature howling in my face, trying to get a rise out of me. My only defense seems to be rattling Annabeth in *their* face, and before you know it, their screams seem a heck of a lot more genuine. Every man and woman here seems to be dressed in an array of gory costumes, and each and every one of them seems to be armed with intimidating modes of weaponry I'm not all that familiar with.

Something blue glows over the small mountain of hay lying out in the distal end of the clearing, and I head that way. God forbid we have a fire on our hands, but as I get closer, I can see it's the moonlight illuminating the landscape. I spot something on the ground in the shape of a person and my heart lurches in my chest.

"It looks like a scarecrow got knocked over," I say to Fish and Sherlock as the din of voices and the music grow increasingly faint the further I get. "Why do I get the feeling this is the only place at the inn without any chaos?"

Sherlock heads over to that scarecrow and lets out a sharp bark. *I think I found chaos, Bizzy.*

I hold up the doll in front of me. "You go first, *Annabelle*," I say, only partly teasing. It's downright creepy out here all by my lonesome, even if I did bring my furry menagerie along. A part of me is expecting a man with a hockey mask to jump out from that mountain of hay and slice my head off.

I make my way over to inspect the human form on the ground, and to my surprise I spot Sprinkles shivering next to that bloodied scarecrow.

"Hey, girl," I say softly. "There's nothing to be afraid of. It's just a silly old scarecrow, see?" I kick it lightly to prove a point, but it feels far more solid than any scarecrow I've ever felt.

The head of the doll in my hand snaps my way, and I'd bet my life her eerie smile just widened a notch.

"*Geez!*" I howl as I hold the haunted thing away from me, and when I do, I happen to see a familiar face looking up from the ground.

A scream gets locked in my throat.

That's no scarecrow.

Lying in a pool of sanguine liquid with a bloody blade nearby is a woman with her face pointed at the sky.

I recognize that blonde hair, that slightly turned-up nose.

It looks as if Blair won't have a chance to teach that rat's hind end a lesson tonight, after all.

Blair Bates is dead.

3

Dead.

Another body in Cider Cove. This can't be happening.

Fish yowls as she jumps from my arms and bolts, while the poor Yorkie shivers uncontrollably.

My eyes quickly survey the scene. Crushed and bloodied hay to the left, footprints that look as if they were engaged in some sort of a struggle all around, the trail of something green that leads further to the field. The moon shines down over it like a spotlight, and I see it for what it is, money, lying everywhere as if it were confetti.

I glance back to Blair, her body slumped over and lifeless, as a glint of something caught in a button at the base of her chest snags my eye. It's a ring—silver with a gold rose. And tucked into the middle of that rose shines a baby blue stone. I glance over to Blair's hand and note her own ring I saw on her earlier is still on her finger. It's an identical replica to this one, with the exception of the color of the gemstone.

Just above her head lies something that gleams white under the moonlight, a hook of some sort. I take a ginger step in that direction to get a better look in the event the killer is lurking in wait, but it's a long white staff. I think I recognize it from earlier, but my brain is on overload, and I can't remember where. And to the right of that lies a shining blade with the film of fresh blood on it. But it's the terror still etched on Blair's face that shakes me, and that scream itching to evict itself from my throat finally does just that.

An entire series of horrific screams wail from me as Sherlock takes off like a bullet, and soon both Jasper and Leo are present, checking Blair's vitals, barking orders into their phones, and along with them a crowd begins to amass.

"Oh my goodness." Camila tries to charge her way to the body, and I hold an arm out to stop her.

"You can't get any closer," I tell her. "You'll destroy evidence that way."

No sooner do I say the words than a deputy cordons off the area with bright yellow caution tape that glows like a menace in this dark area of the meadow.

"I can't believe this is happening," Camila pants as her skin grows pale, and suddenly, Camila looks as if she's ready to pass out.

That trio of Camila's friends I met earlier press to the front of the crowd as they make their way over.

"Oh no!" Sabrina cries out. "*Blair!*" she screams, and the pain on her face is visceral. Her pale gray eyes glow in the moonlight, giving her all the appeal of a supernatural being. She wraps her arms around herself, and that snakeskin painted onto her flesh looks as if it's morphed into the real deal and I'm forced to look away.

Raven, the one with long black hair, dressed as a vampire, does her best to comfort the girl.

"It's okay," she pants. ***It's all over. It's done. It's finally done. I can't believe this.***

My eyes widen as I look her way. Curious thoughts.

What's done? The *murder*?

The girl dressed as a librarian, Tabitha I think her name is, takes a stiff step forward. She looks as if she were in a trance as her gaze is set on the lifeless woman lying on the hay.

The blame needs to go somewhere. She looks in my direction, and my mouth falls open ready to refute it.

"You did this." Her voice comes out weak as she looks my way. "You killed her. I saw you coming here alone. You did this!" Her voice hikes to the sky, and I shake my head—my own voice unable to mobilize.

"No." It comes out in a puff of air as she comes in close.

"You did this!" she riots so loud that the attention of every soul in the vicinity is forced to look in this direction. "I saw you with my own two eyes, Camila!"

"Camila?" I say her name with an air of surprise as I turn to look at the accused standing directly behind me.

Camila's eyes reflect the moonlight, and the sheer terror on her face reflects that of the one on the deceased.

"I didn't do it, I swear," she pumps out the words in a fury.

A thought hits me as I glance down at her Bo Peep costume.

"That staff." I point to the crime scene. "Is that yours?"

Sabrina pants, "It is!" One of her snakelike arms pulls me back as she steps closer to Camila. "You were arguing with her. We all heard it."

"That's right," Raven snaps. "Blair suggested you find someplace private to speak. This is where you took her, isn't it?"

"No." Camila shakes her head in a panic just as Jasper and Leo step up next to me, and now all three of us are riveted at attention along with the rest of the crowd as the accusations fly. "I mean, yes." Camila presses her fingers to her temple. "We stepped over here." She points back to where the money and the footprints singe the ground. "And we—we were talking, but I didn't *kill* her."

"You weren't talking," Tabitha snaps. "I followed you. I heard you tell her that you had enough. And once I heard the two of you going at it, I took off to get the others." The whites of her eyes glint as she looks to Raven and Sabrina.

"Jasper"—Camila's eyes bulge as she reaches for him, and there's a distinct dark crimson streak along the back of her right hand—"you have to believe me. I didn't do this. I'm not capable of murder. I would never hurt anybody."

"*Your hand*," Sabrina screams. "You have her blood on it!"

Jasper glances down, and instantly the disappointment is ripe on his face.

He blows out a breath. "I'm sorry, Camila. I'm going to have to ask you a few questions, and we're going to need to take a sample of that blood on your hand."

"What?" Camila shrieks as she examines herself in the moonlight.

"*Leo*," Jasper barks. "I'm going to ask you to take Camila in. I'll button up as quick as I can and meet you down in Seaview."

Leo escorts a hysterical Camila off into the night, and her incessant cries of innocence are heard with every step of the way.

"Jasper"—I whisper as he pulls me away from the crowd for a moment—"do you really think Camila is capable of murder?"

"I don't know." He shakes his head, his eyes wild with shock. "I suppose everyone is capable of murder if pushed in the right direction. Why don't you help close up shop? I don't think anyone needs to be on the grounds tonight."

"I will," I say. "I saw something," I pant. "I saw footprints to the left—and lots of money."

He glances that way. "I saw that, too."

"Did you see the ring? There's a ring on Blair's shirt. It's caught on her button. It could belong to the killer." I shake my head. "Or it could be Blair's. I really don't know."

He leans in a notch. "Bizzy, did you know this girl?"

"No, we just met, but I can tell you everything I know about her so far. And the things she was thinking." I nod his way.

"Okay. Go ahead and get this show shut down. It looks like I'll have to head to the station as soon as we finish up here, but we'll talk." He presses an urgent kiss to my lips.

We pull away and I can't help but make a face. "It's been quite a homecoming, hasn't it?"

"It's not what anyone wanted." He pulls back and gets a better look at the doll I'm holding. "*Geez.*" He takes a full step back. "Is that a prop or something?"

"It's our lovechild, Annabeth." I wrinkle my nose at the thing. "She belongs to Georgie. And believe me, I'd like nothing more than to give her back. I'll herd the masses to the exit. Hopefully, this gets resolved quickly." I dot another kiss to his lips and a thought hits me. "Oh! That dog!"

"What dog?" He searches my face.

"Blair's dog." I point over at the poor thing still shivering right where I found her. "Can I take her? I'll make sure she's safe."

"You bet." Jasper disappears for less than ten seconds before he lands the shivering cutie into my arms. "Be safe, Bizzy." He glances past me into the crowd. "If Camila didn't do it, that means the killer is still out there. And if they are, I'd bet money they were watching the scene unfold." He takes off, and I step to the side with that tiny baby in my arms.

"It's okay," I whisper to the sweet little cutie. "You're safe. I've got you. And do you know what? I can hear your thoughts and understand you. It's sort of an odd little quirk of mine."

She lets out a sharp bark. *Is it true? Is my Blair gone?*

"I'm sorry." I plant a kiss on her head. "It's terrible news, I know. Did you happen to see who did this to her?"

My word, this tiny shivering furball might just be the key to this entire murder investigation.

I didn't see it. She whimpers. *That woman was talking to Blair, and I was set on the ground. I began to wander. I could smell the tracks of many*

45

animals, and I wanted a fresh patch to relieve myself on so I went toward the woods. I heard voices, though—angry, heated voices. And I heard footsteps, too. Lots and lots of footsteps.

"Lots of footsteps? Like more than one person?"

Oh yes. From different people. Footsteps are like voices, too, you know. Each person makes a different sound when they take a step.

"Of course." *Huh.* That might just be the saving grace for Camila after all, unless, of course, she confesses. I'm not Camila's biggest fan, but I'd like to make sure the *right* person is put away for this heinous crime.

I get straight to the job of evicting every last soul from the property with the help of both Emmie and Jordy. And it's nothing short of mass hysteria as people scream their way back onto the main road.

"Bizzy!" a couple of female voices call out my name at once, and I spot both Juni and Georgie headed this way.

Juni looks as if she's dressed like a biker chick in a short leather skirt and matching bustier, but then that is her go-to look when she's going out for the evening, so I doubt any effort was put into a costume.

Juni, *Juniper Moonbeam*, is Georgie's look-alike daughter, save for the fact she has less gray hair, less wrinkles, and quite possibly less good sense. They do, however, share the same devilish gleam in their sparkling blue eyes and same penchant for trouble. Juni has a broad forehead, slender long nose, and mostly dark blonde hair.

Georgie gasps for air as if she's just run a lap around the entire property, and she just might have.

"I found Fish by the gate and Sherlock, too, so I took them back to my place and shut them in for the night," she screeches.

"Thank you," I tell her.

"I can't believe you found another one, Bizzy." Juni growls out a dark laugh. "You can't tell me that body didn't wait for you to get back from your honeymoon."

"Well, it did," I snip as I shove the haunted doll I've been carting around for the better part of the night into Georgie's hands. "And it looks as if Camila might have had something to do with this."

"*What?*" Georgie howls and inadvertently rattles Annabeth, forcing the doll's eyes to click open and shut at a frenetic—might I add, haunted rate. And it's an unnerving sight. "I knew it, Bizzy. A girl who's willing to kill a relationship with someone as dangerously handsome as Jasper Wilder is capable of anything."

"I say good riddance." Juni slaps her hands as if wiping them clean.

"Wait." I squeeze my eyes shut because what's about to come next isn't something I say with ease. "We don't know for sure if she did it. She might be innocent."

Sprinkles lets out a sharp bark. *She had blood on her hands. And she had that tall weapon she was wielding.*

"Was she wielding that staff as a weapon?" I ask as I look at the tiny sweetheart in my arms.

I saw it myself, Bizzy.

Juni grunts, "It looks as if Little Bo Peep is about to find some new sheep to play with—in the slammer."

"I don't know," I say as I look out at the crowd quickly draining off the property. "I think I might just have to dig a little deeper before they lock her up and throw away the key." But maybe not too deep. This is Camila we're talking about.

"Hear that, Annabeth?" Georgie rattles the haunted doll, making her eyes open and close at a quickened clip once again. "Hold onto your curls, Red. We've got an investigation coming up ahead."

I nod her way.

"And something tells me, it's going to be a bumpy ride," I whisper.

The sky rumbles as a dark boil of clouds sweeps in quick like the steam floating off a cauldron.

She's dead. A voice calls out from somewhere behind me, and I turn, looking into the frightened faces of those slow to exit.

When I'm not standing near the person whose mind is open to me, their voice sounds more or less androgynous. And right about now, I really wish it didn't.

Blair Bates was right. She will be taking her secret to the grave. And I just made it happen.

A breath hitches in my throat as I do my best to search the masses for a single familiar face, but I don't see one.

"I don't think Camila killed Blair Bates," I pant. "I think the killer is still here among us."

A jag of lightning goes off in the sky, illuminating that doll in Georgie's hand a strange shade of green, and yet once the sky retreats to its darkened state, that strange green glow remains.

Juni and Georgie howl and scream as the doll in Georgie's arms turns her head my way and gives a sly wink.

A scream of my own gets locked in my throat.

As if a murder wasn't enough to rattle me, that haunted doll just took the haunted cake.

But in truth, on a night like this, it feels as if all of Cider Cove is haunted.

I did it. That distant internal voice goes off again.

And I just got away with murder.

"No, you didn't," I whisper. "Nobody gets away with murder on my watch."

4

October is bringing with it everything this horror-based month has promised, chilly winds that blow the leaves right off the trees, an overabundance of pumpkins that dot the landscape as far as the eye can see, hayrides, hay *fever*, and icy cold terror that lays over our small town like a dark, ominous cloud.

The dark clouds were indeed out in full force this morning as I took Fish, Sherlock Bones, and our new tiny addition, Sprinkles, out for a walk along the cove. The sandy beaches are barren this time of year, save for a few of the guests of the inn trying to soak in any part of the majestic Atlantic they can sink their feet into.

The ocean reflects the sky in both hue and anger this morning, dark and unknowable like a monster rousing from its slumber.

Afterwards, I drop into the Country Cottage Café and pick up a few strips of bacon for both Sherlock Bones and Sprinkles—and for Fish, a few quick licks of milk from a saucer I keep in the kitchen office just for her. The café is connected to the back of the inn with a full covered patio that looks out at the majestic Atlantic. Emmie is in charge of the kitchen and predominantly does all of the baking, which is exactly why this place is such a hit with both the tourists and the guests alike.

Thank you, Bizzy, Fish mewls. *I needed every last creamy sip. I didn't get a wink of sleep with these two in the living room last night.*

"You could have slept with me," I say. Fish's favorite place to catch some shut-eye is right on top of my head. And she has an unusual knack for waking me up at the crack of dawn with a whip of her tail to my face. And for that reason alone, I haven't bothered with an alarm since I've had her.

I'm not sleeping with you, until you kick Jasper out of the bedroom. She twitches her whiskers my way.

Sherlock barks at the thought. *She's not kicking Jasper anywhere. You're going to have to get used to him. Just like you're going to have to get used to me, kitten.*

Sprinkles lets out a yippy string of barks. *And what about me? How do I live anywhere without Blair?*

"Oh, Sprinkles." I give her back a little rub. "Rest assured, you'll stay with me until I can contact her family."

They won't want me. They hardly wanted her. I don't think she had a mother, and her father is always cruising—whatever that means.

"It means he's on the high seas and he can't have a pet."

My father happens to be cruising at the moment as well. He's engaged to Jasper's mother—a long and rather baffling story. Anyway, once Jasper and I left for our honeymoon, we got a text from the two of them saying they were going to take a honeymoon of their own. Words that sponsored visuals that I never wanted to have. They'll be gone until November, living up the highlife with midnight buffets and reading books by the pool. I won't lie. That aspect of it leaves me more than a tiny bit envious.

"But don't worry, Sprinkles," I say. "You can stay with me for as long as you need to. And you'll have Fish and Sherlock to keep you company, and play with."

I like to play, Fish says, lashing Sprinkles over the face with her tail.

Sherlock gives a light growl. *Don't let her get away with anything, Sprinkles. The next thing you know, it'll be your head she's sleeping on. I should know, it's happened to me.* He lets out another bark. *Come on, let's go check out that haunted doll collection of Georgie's. I heard from a rat that those things were*

glowing and floating through the air last night when everyone went to sleep.

The three of them take off, and I scoff in their wake.

"Wait a minute—we don't have rats," I call after them and three different customers look my way.

Do we have rats?

I make a beeline over to the ballroom. I've yet to see this haunted doll collection that Georgie has cursed the inn with. I've never been afraid of a doll. I've never collected them either. Most of the tiny human replicas I acquired were castoffs of my sisters. And by the time Macy was through with them, they had been given lopsided haircuts, had their entire hands painted with nail polish, and had their feet chewed off. I'm not sure why Macy had a habit of chewing on her dolls' feet, but my mother always said it was better than chewing on her own.

Speaking of my mother and Macy...

"Bizzy!" My mother meets up with me just as I'm about to crest the threshold into the ballroom. She's quick to collapse her arms around me, and I'm forced to take in her thick perfume. My mother's perfume has been the same since I was a child, and it's always reminded me of strong tea. "Oh, tell me you didn't do this."

She shakes her head with a touch of disappointment in her clear blue eyes. Ree Baker is a headstrong, confident woman who more or less raised her three children on her own once she untangled herself from my father. He went on to marry everything that moved, and she went on to run a real estate empire that to this day is going strong even though she's been retired from the company for years now. Her caramel blonde hair touches her shoulders and is feathered back like the ode to the eighties it is. She's petite, and in shape, and I can only aspire to be every bit like her one day.

Macy grunts as she rolls her eyes, "Don't admit to anything, Biz." She elbows my mother. Macy dyes her black hair blonde and has icy blue eyes that match her icy blue soul. "Remember what I said. We don't want to get on her bad side. Face it, Mom. You raised a killer."

"*Macy.*" I shake my head as I give a quick glance around. "I don't know who did this. But I do know it wasn't me."

Emmie bops up with a platter of those jack-o'-lantern hand pies and a witch's hat on her head. "Bizzy Baker *Wilder.* You know very well who did it. Leo told me everything." My bestie leans toward my mother and sister with a look of unmitigated glee in her eyes. "It was Camila Ryder. Leo says they found blood evidence on her hands and that she beat the poor victim with her staff before bludgeoning her to death."

Macy gasps, her mouth rounding out with a smile. "*Camila*, Camila? Jasper's raunchy ex?" She scoops up a hand pie for herself.

"Yes," I say, picking up a hand pie myself, as does my mother. "*Camila*, Camila. But she didn't really do this. It just looks bad. And Jasper says the woman was stabbed. They found the knife at the scene."

Emmie frowns my way. "You keep out of this. Camila was Leo's ex, too, you know. And it's as if nothing can keep her from sniffing around either one of them. I'm sick of her trying to steal my man." *Especially since I'm sniffing around Leo myself—hoping to find a ring in his pocket someday soon.*

My eyes round out at the matrimonial-based thought.

Emmie must really think Leo is the one for her.

My heart sinks a little because I know the inevitable is at hand. Leo is about to let her in on his little mind-reading secret, and that means I'm about to do the same.

My stomach knots up just thinking about it.

Mom moans as she shakes her head my way. "I know that look on your face, Bizzy. You don't plan on staying out of this at all. I don't approve of *that* at all. You've almost gotten yourself killed before, poking your nose where it doesn't belong."

My lips press tight a moment. "Don't worry about me. Jasper is on the case, and we've worked together before. I'm going to be just fine, I promise you. *Everything* is going to be fine."

A shrill scream goes off deep in the ballroom and the four of us try to head inside, but Jordy has the entry roped off.

"Six bucks apiece." He sheds his signature toothy smile. "Sorry, ladies. Georgie makes the rules. I just keep them."

"That's funny," I say. "Because I dole out your paycheck." I gasp as I take a quick look around at the bevy of round tables set out, each one with a creepy looking doll encased in glass dotting the center of it. "Wow. I have a feeling I'm going to have to hire an exorcist once we clear this place out. Let me through, Jordy."

He glowers a moment as he swipes a hand pie off his sister's plate.

"Rules are rules." He gives a lazy grin before biting into the tasty treat he just scooped up.

"Let me guess." I squint his way. "Georgie is splitting her take with you?"

His lips cinch, telling me everything I need to know.

"Oh, for Pete's sake." My mother fishes a few bills out of her purse and forks them over. "Keep the change. My grandmother used to collect dolls, and I'm dying to see what you've got here." She takes another hand pie before looking my way. "Keep out of trouble, kid. If you find one more body, it's *you* I'm taking straight to the exorcist."

She takes off as Emmie extends the tray of hand pies.

"I'll be making the rounds, offering up a quick bite to all the guests." Emmie wrinkles her nose. "After last night, I think all of Cider Cove deserves a hand pie."

"And a shot of tequila," Macy quips.

She takes off as Macy and I follow her into the exhibit.

It's one thing to see these inanimate faces from afar, but to see them up close is both jarring and frightful. Some dolls have long, elaborate curls, while some are shorn to the quick. Some faces are pristine and beautiful, while others have dark circles under their eyes, pale clay faces, broken noses, and significant skull fractures. And yet, there are just as many rag dolls as there are otherwise, even a few Raggedy Ann and Andy dolls, which I happen to be a very big fan of. In fact, I've still got a small one sitting on my dresser back in my cottage. My grandmother gave it to me, and I've kept it in view ever since just to remind me of her.

"I think I'm going to need that tequila," I say as Macy links her arm to mine and pulls me in close.

"Don't worry, Bizzy. Once the spirits decide to burn down this entire inn, I'll have a bottle delivered to your room at the insane asylum."

"You're not funny," I say.

"I'm not trying to be."

We walk along from table to table and, interestingly enough, each doll has a name plate and a brief history provided.

"Look at that," Macy muses. "These dolls are ancient. Doesn't Georgie know that ancient artifacts haul evil curses around with them? You'd better thank your unlucky stars she didn't land a mummy in the middle of the room."

Just then a tornado of a body waves and jumps as she runs right up to us.

It's Georgie Conner herself clad in a pumpkin orange kaftan, her hair a touch more unruly than it usually is.

"Great news, Bizzy! Freddie says we can have the mummy, too! It's being delivered this afternoon, and we're going to put it smack-dab in the middle of the room. Of course, the prices will have to go up for the exhibit. I'm thinking twenty bucks a pop. Don't worry, Bizzy. I'll send them all to the café once they're through here. Don't think for a minute I didn't learn a thing or two from our friends in Honey Hollow."

My mouth opens, but not a word comes out as I give pause to my thought.

My transmundane friend out in Honey Hollow, Lottie Lemon—well, her mother owns and runs a haunted B&B where she offers tours for *eighty* dollars a head of her spooktacular abode. Then when she's through with the people, she sends them all to Lottie's bakery for what she calls The Last Thing They Ate Tour. It seems Lottie has the same knack for stumbling upon bodies that I do. Only with Lottie, one of her desserts always seems to turn up at the scene of the crime. It's a wonder she hasn't been arrested yet.

Heck, it's a wonder *I* haven't been arrested yet.

"Don't worry about sending the guests to the café," I tell her.

Macy groans. "Don't you listen to her, Georgie. You send them to the café, and then you make sure they head to the Lather and Light right afterwards, too. I'm running a buy one-get one special on all fall scented *boo*-ble baths. You should both come by. The pumpkin pie and apple cider scents are to die for." She belts out a maniacal laugh, and Georgie snaps her fingers.

"That's exactly what this place is missing." Georgie slaps my sister on the back. "A little *mood* music. I'll ask Jordy to hook me up with those haunted beats he had playing at the frightmare. And don't you worry, Bizzy. I talked to Leo this morning, and he said we can start up again as soon as tonight as long as we keep that area off-limits."

"What? No," I say just as Juni and a dark-haired man clad in black join us. He's tall, thin, about thirty, has dark amber eyes that glint red in the light, and he's wearing an eerie grin reminiscent of one of these creepy dolls.

"I found him, Mama." Juni smacks the man on the stomach. "And he's ready to meet our demands."

Macy gurgles out a dark laugh, and judging by the glazed look in her eyes, she likes what she sees. "Never mind meeting their demands. I think you'll be much more interested in *mine*." She holds out her hand and he shakes it. "Macy Baker, psychic extraordinaire. I can see the future— and yours just so happens to be with me. At least it is tonight. Please tell me you're free for dinner."

Macy is no psychic, but she's a maneater, and she's apparently very hungry today.

His dark, pointed brows hike a notch, but his lids hood, giving the answer for him before his lips could get there.

His lips flicker. "Only if you allow me to pick up the tab."

Georgie grunts, "All right, you two, cool it before I tell Annabeth to go fetch me a cup of water to dump over your heads. Bizzy, Macy, this is my good friend, Freddie Dodd. He's the curator over at Madame Tarantula's Museum of the Odd and Curious down in Ellsworth. He's the one I bribed to let me have the haunted doll collection for the entire month of October."

"Just the last thirteen days." He winks over at Macy. "And I don't accept bribes."

"Fine." Georgie shrugs. "All I had to do was flash my boobs. I'm telling you, Bizzy. They've been hermetically sealed for so long I've still got a set to impress." She smacks Freddie on the arm. "Tell it like it is, kid."

"Truer words were never spoken." He chuckles. "But all you would have had to do is ask. I would do anything for you, Georgie."

Macy bounces her shoulders his way. "How about me? Would you do anything for me, Freddie boy?"

A dark laugh strums from him as he stares right into my sister's baby blue eyes.

"I'm no boy," he warns her. "I'm all man. But I suppose a woman as beautiful as you demands actions, not words."

"Be at the Lather and Light on Main Street at seven and we'll take it from there," she's quick to close the deal. "I have a feeling you'll enjoy exactly where you end up at the end of the night."

"All right," I say. "Dinner and *you* for dessert. We get it." I make a face at the man before us. "Freddie, these dolls aren't really haunted, are they?"

He gives a quick look around, the smile quickly dissipating from his lips.

"Let's just say they have a certain history. I'm not sure about most of them, but I know for a fact one is very, *very* haunted." He offers Georgie a hard stare. "My love, where is Annabeth? I swept the room twice, and I've yet to see her."

Georgie gasps as she clutches at her chest. "I set her right in that glass box last night before I went to bed. Just the way you told me to."

Juni tips her head to the side. "And I swear on my life, she was just there. Or at least she was when I got here earlier."

Freddie scowls as he looks toward a table to his left, and I note the empty glass box sitting there with the door sealed shut.

"She's gone now," he says. "Georgie, I gave you explicit instructions. You must keep Annabeth locked in that glass case the entire duration that the exhibit is here. It's pertinent no one must touch her, lest the darkness within her unleashes on that poor unsuspecting soul."

"I touched her!" Georgie howls. "Oh, help me, Juni!" she cries. "I need to see a woman about some sage." She hauls her daughter off so fast, they nearly knock over six displays in the process.

"I don't really believe any of that," I'm quick to tell him. "I touched her, too."

His eyes ride up and down my body. "I'd be careful if I were you. She prefers pretty girls, and you seem to fit the bill."

"She prefers pretty girls for what?" I shake my head at the nonsense.

Freddie frowns. "Don't mock what you know nothing about. The doll is wicked. And I promise, you don't want to find out any more than that."

"Well, I call malarkey." I don't mind one bit calling him out for trying to scare any of us. "And when that toy does show up, I'll be sure to put her right back where she belongs. There's not a thing she or any trumped-up wickedness can do to me."

The lights flicker in the room as the sound of roaring thunder cuts through the walls.

"It's too late." Macy moans as she clutches onto my arm with a death grip. "She's already coming for you, Bizzy, and she's going to eat the rest of us, too."

"She is not going to eat anybody," I say, although with not as much conviction I had a moment ago.

And just like that, the lights go out in the ballroom, leaving us in a den of darkness. A few gasps and screams go off, and I can hear Jordy shouting that he'll turn on the generator.

My phone goes off, and the light of the screen momentarily blinds me.

It's a text from Emmie.

Electrical storm knocked out power all over Cider Cove. And FYI, just talked to Leo a few minutes ago. Camila hasn't been arrested yet. She's already back at work, trying to flirt her way into his heart. Why do I get the feeling she has the entire Seaview Sheriff's Department wrapped around her

finger? Let's just hope they don't let her get away with murder.

I quickly text back. **She won't. How about you and I deliver some hand pies down to the station and say hello to our men just to make it clear to her they're taken?**

My phone blinks back to life as Emmie texts right back. **I'm already packing up a box.**

The lights come back on, and a weak applause circles the room. I glance to that empty glass case where Annabeth should be sitting and frown.

There's no way that doll had anything to do with the fact the lights went out. Just like Camilla didn't have anything to do with Blair Bates' murder.

I'm sorry, *Annabelle*, but you don't frighten me one bit.

The lights flicker again, and this time they can't seem to stop.

A chill runs up my spine, and it makes me wonder about Annabeth, about Camila.

What if I'm wrong on both counts?

What if I'm about to help someone get away with murder?

5

The Seaview Sheriff's Department sits like a dull gray cube under an equally dull gray sky. A few pumpkins are set out front, and inside there are pictures of ghosts holding cauldrons full of Halloween candy with the words, *Don't get tricked. Bring your treats in to be inspected!*

For a kid, I'm pretty sure there would be nothing more terrifying on Halloween than heading down to the sheriff's station to have your candy x-rayed for razors. Talk about a hair-raising way to end a hair-raising night. Although I'm not sure it would hamper my appetite for the sweet stuff either.

Emmie and I mobilized quickly. She not only boxed up one platter of jack-o'-lantern hand pies, she boxed up *three*. One for Leo, one for Jasper, and one for Camila in hopes to get her to talk. Camila might be roaming the streets as a free woman again, but that doesn't mean that good time will last for long.

I brought Sprinkles along for the ride. I figured if the hand pies weren't enough to get Camila to cough up a few details about her twisted friends, maybe looking into the eyes of this adorable little Yorkie would do the trick.

Truth be told, this little cutie could get me to do just about anything. But then again, I have a heart, and whether that functioning organ exists inside of Camila's body is still up for debate. And once Sherlock Bones saw me leashing Sprinkles up, he promised to behave if I took him to see Jasper at work—and well, it turns out, I can't deny Sherlock Bones anything either. Then, like the falling of the final domino, Fish somehow ended up in a tote bag that sits on my shoulder, peeking her fuzzy little head out as we make our way over to the homicide division.

Emmie leans in. "Let me talk to Camila first. We have less friction in our relationship." *But so help me God, if that woman so much as looks at my man sideways again, she'll be feeling some major friction, all right—with my fist.*

A tiny laugh bubbles in me.

Emmie is the last person to resort to physical violence, but people seem to be a lot more animated in their mind than they come across in real life—and thankfully so.

We spot the abomination of desolation seated in the holy of holies—her desk situated right across from Jasper's office. I can't help but frown at her.

Camila's hot pink lips glow against her perennially tan skin. Her hair surrounds her like a majestic chestnut-colored lion's mane, and she's wearing a cute cowl neck sweater dress in the perfect shade of burnt orange just for fall.

She glances up momentarily before getting back to her work.

"What now?" she snips.

"We're here to turn that frown upside down." Emmie opens a box of her to die for jack-o'-lantern hand pies and slides it across Camila's desk. "We were just popping in to see our men"—*as in not yours*—"and thought we'd bring you a few treats to brighten your mood."

"Yeah," I say, quickly scooping up Sprinkles into my arms, aka my secret weapon of cuteness, and positioning her just right so Camila can take a gander at all the adorable fuzzy wonder. "And look who's here to say hello?" I wave over at her with one of Sprinkles' paws.

Sherlock nuzzles his way around my knees. *Don't tell her I'm here, Bizzy. The woman is a shrew. Leo himself said so once. And even though I'm not entirely sure what a shrew is, I think he's right.*

My lips twitch because Leo has never been more right.

Fish lets out a tiny mewl. *I don't care what she thinks about me. I'm going to stare her down until she's too uncomfortable to look at me. If I were her cat, I'd glare at her all day long.*

"I don't care about Blair's fleabag." Camila snaps up a hand pie and snarls our way.

Sprinkles huffs, *Well, I certainly don't care for her either. Especially not after the way I saw her treating my Blair. All of that yelling and screaming, I could tell right away she wasn't a very nice woman.*

Thanks to Sprinkles, I know for a fact they argued.

"I'm still the number one suspect," Camila grunts through a bite. "I may be free for now, but Jasper suggested I lawyer up. That was my staff they found behind her body, and I know for a fact it will have *my* fingerprints on it."

Emmie leans in. "What about that blood on your hand?"

Camila gives a sideways glance. "Well, it wasn't my blood. They're running tests. But I swear on my grandmother's grave, if it comes back that it belonged to Blair, I'm going to find whoever is setting me up, and then I'm going to murder them." Her eyes flash with fire as she sheds a wicked grin, and all three pets whimper on cue. I can't blame them. I'm half-tempted myself.

"All right, Camila," I say. "You have to tell me everything you know about what happened last night. If you didn't kill her, who do you think did?"

"I'm sorry." She leans back with a semi-amused expression on her face. "Did I miss the part where you flashed your badge my way and told me I was about to undergo an interrogation?"

Emmie scoffs over at her. "I can't believe you. If there is one woman who can prove your innocence, it's this one. If I were you, I'd be more than a little grateful she would even bother having a conversation with you after the way you've treated her. Everyone knows Bizzy is better at tracking down a killer than every homicide detective and sheriff's deputy in this building combined."

Someone clears their throat from behind, and we turn to find both Jasper and Leo shedding wry smiles.

"Oh." Emmie gasps. "Hand pie?" She's quick to land a box in each of their hands before smacking Leo on the lips with a kiss. "Now where exactly is this new office of yours? I don't believe we've christened it properly." She whisks Leo off, and I'm left to wonder why I haven't christened Jasper's office just yet myself.

"Detective." I bite down on a smile as I look up at my handsome husband. "Care for a hand pie?"

"In a bit." His brows furrow. "What's going on?" He offers Sherlock a quick pat.

He's onto you, Bizzy! Sherlock barks. *That's my Jasper. Nothing gets past him.*

Fish lets out a tiny hiss. *You mean nothing gets past Bizzy. She's always ten steps ahead of him.*

Sprinkles whimpers. *I bet that's why he's lost his appetite for hand pies.*

Camila taps her pen against her notebook in an effort to garner our attention.

"I'm afraid it was me she came to see, Jasper. It seems your little wifey is obsessed with playing the whodunit game."

I scoff over at her. "Is that what you call your freedom? A *game*? Good luck to you then." I look to Jasper with a new resolve as I raise my right hand. "I, Bizzy Baker Wilder, hereby solemnly swear that I will not inject myself into Blair Bates' homicide investigation. I will not trace a suspect. And should I bump into one in the wild, I will refrain from questioning them in any capacity that might lead me on the path to find the killer." I turn my head toward Camila. "Contrary to popular opinion, I prefer to leave the investigative side of life to my perfectly capable husband. Now if you'll excuse us, we've got an office to christen."

Jasper's lips curve at the thought. "Now that's something I can get behind." He navigates my entire menagerie and me inside his office, seals the door shut, and instantly I'm ensconced with the heady scent of his cologne.

Jasper's office isn't all too exciting—beige walls, brown desk, black leather chair, and a picture of a dog with a police cap hangs on the wall. But with Jasper standing within these four walls, there's no place on earth that could be more exciting.

"Hey there, Detective." I give a little wink as I land Sprinkles to the floor. "I'm not sure where one starts with a christening." I give his tie a firm tug.

His lids hood as he pulls me close. "I've got a pretty good idea." He lands his lips to mine and makes me forget all about the homicide investigation at hand, Camila, and basically the rest of planet Earth.

Sherlock lets out a sharp bark. ***Close your eyes, Sprinkles. Things might get messy. Jasper hasn't learned how to lick her face yet. I keep showing him how to do it and he keeps forgetting.***

Sprinkles chirps. ***And here I thought Blair was the unteachable one. Go figure. Don't worry. I won't hold it against him.***

Fish groans. ***Bizzy won't listen either. The least she could do is groom his hair with a few good licks. But it's as if she hardly cares for the poor man.***

I scoff as I pull away from the dreamy kiss at hand.

"I very much care for Jasper," I say, making a face at the furry trio. "Sorry." I shrug up at Jasper. "There was a runaway conversation I felt I needed to butt into."

He curls his lips on one side as he examines the furry-laden among us. "Why do I get the feeling christening my office will prove to be a challenge with six pairs of eyes on the prowl?"

"Because you're a very good detective."

"That's not what Emmie thinks."

"Emmie has questionable judgment, as evidenced by the carnival she's running at the inn." I run my finger down his chest. "And lucky for you, you're married to *me*. I have all the faith in the world you're going to crack this case right open. You've got this."

A half-smile cinches on his cheek and gives him that lethally sexy look I fell for so hard in the beginning. I'm still falling for it.

"You made an oath out there, Mrs. Wilder, and I heard it. I plan on holding you to it. You're right, I've got this. But that has nothing to do with my ego. Instead, it has everything to do with the fact I need you safe. This is a dangerous case. I'll make sure that the harvest festival—especially that frightmare has plenty of deputies roaming the grounds."

"*Ooh.* Can they dress up as zombies? I sort of have a thing for gun-toting men in tattered clothes."

"Funny you should mention that. I happen to own a pair of holey jeans, and I like to pack heat."

"I also find gun-toting men who vacuum and do the dishes exceptionally hot as well." I bite down on my lower lip to keep that smile from breaking free on my face.

A dark laugh strums in his chest. "Smooth, real smooth."

His phone chirps and his features harden on a dime. "The results came back for that blood work found on Camila's hand."

I suck in a quick breath. "Well?"

Jasper's chest widens with his next breath. "It was Blair's."

We head out and Jasper spills the bloody beans to Camila.

"*What?*" Her eyes grow large. A genuine look of fright takes over her face, and if I'm not mistaken, her hands are trembling. "That's not possible." She rises out of her seat and makes her way around the desk.

Look out, Bizzy! Sherlock jumps between us. *She's headed your way, and she's capable of murder.* He barks up at Jasper. *Don't just stand there. Arrest the woman!*

Sprinkles whines and whimpers. *She killed my Blair, and now she's coming after us all.*

Sprinkles howls. *We're gonna end up in the morgue!*

Oh, brother. Fish moans. ***Jasper has a gun. Bizzy has her wit. And I have my claws. The two of you shivering canines can relax. Nobody ends up in the morgue today.***

Jasper nods my way. "I need to get over to forensics. There are a few things I need to discuss with them. I'll try to be home early. I can bring takeout."

"And I'll offer up dessert." I waggle my brows so he knows exactly which sweet treat he'll be biting into.

He dots my lips with a kiss before tucking his lips to my ear. "Just FYI, I like my dessert naked." He winks as he takes off and Fish yowls in his wake.

Where is he going? Fish does her best to stand up straight. ***Bizzy, quick, leave. We can't be alone with this maniac. Oh goodness, we're all going to end up in the morgue.***

Camila wastes no time in gripping me by the arms and giving me a slight shake.

"You have to help, Bizzy. I can't go away for murder one. Especially not for a murder I didn't commit."

My mouth falls open as I take a step back. "Unlike the one you got away with? Don't worry. You've got Jasper by your side. He'll take good care of you." Words I never thought I'd speak to Camila Ryder.

She chokes and gags. "Are you kidding me? I don't care if I have this entire department by my side. I don't want any of them. I want you." Her eyes sharpen over mine. "And I want you to make this go away as quickly as possible. I mean it, Bizzy. I'm ready to let bygones be bygones between us. I'll do whatever it takes to clear my name."

"Obviously." I frown over at her. "But I wish you would have said something earlier. I gave Jasper my word."

"Well un-word yourself. The corpse just hit the fan, and I need a seasoned pro."

Don't do it. Sherlock nuzzles his head against my leg. ***Jasper is right. This is a dangerous case.***

My heart starts to race at the thought of stepping back into the investigative game. I can't help it. Some girls are addicted to coffee and chocolate; I'm addicted to coffee and chocolate with a side of murder. I'll have some explaining to do to Jasper. But let's be honest. At this point in our lives, he pretty much expects it.

"Okay, fine," I say as I give a quick glance around. "We'll have to talk in-depth about it. But not here. In the meantime, I want you to try to remember every detail about last night."

"Name the time and the place. I'll sing like a bird. I can come to work late if that helps."

"Perfect. Meet me at the inn tomorrow morning at nine." That way, Jasper will be safely in Seaview.

"Tomorrow at nine." She takes a deep breath. ***I feel better already. And as much as I can't bring myself*** *to say it out loud, I mean it.* She nods my way with the thought.

I give a little wink her way before collecting my menagerie and my slightly disheveled bestie and heading back to Cider Cove.

That night Jasper picks up dinner just like he said, and I offer up myself as dessert as promised. No sooner do we make our way into the bedroom and flick on the lights than a scream works its way up my throat.

Good news and bad news.

The good news? Annabeth is no longer missing.

The bad news? She's sitting in the middle of my bed, hugging my very own Raggedy Ann doll.

"There's a note," Jasper says as we both lean in to view the tiny white square of parchment on Annabeth's dress.

It reads, *Stay out of it, or you're next, Busy.*

6

The Country Cottage Inn is bustling, especially after experiencing another night flooded with monsters on the prowl at the frightmare attraction. But lucky for me, this morning seems to be filled with throngs of mothers, all of which have adorable costumed toddlers in tow as they head to the beach to pick out the perfect pumpkin to call their own.

Camila darkens my doorway right at nine on the button, and I leave the front desk in the capable hands of my co-workers, Grady and Nessa, a couple of recent college grads that help run this place.

"Where to?" Camila asks as I head around the counter. "The café to nosh on the calorie dense offerings?"

And don't think I missed the sarcasm in her voice.

"No, I think I'll spare you the clogged arteries and sugar high. Instead, I'll take you to the ballroom where I'll clog your mind with enough scary porcelain faces to ensure many a nightmare in your near future."

"Please"—she grunts—"that grisly scene the other night already promised to do just that."

We head for the ballroom, and both Sherlock and Sprinkles run off before us. Fish is fast asleep on the reception counter and I don't dare wake her. She's not exactly a morning kitty. Once she has her breakfast, she gets right back to the most important part of her day, sleeping. I know they say it's a dog's life, but I'm pretty sure it's a cat's life, too.

We meet up with Jordy at the roped off entry, and his eyes widen at the sight of Camila. Jordy and Camila dated off and on, but I'm not entirely sure what came of it. But I'm one hundred percent sure I don't want to know the dirty details.

"Well, look who's here." He sheds a dimpled grin her way. *The exact person my bed has been missing.* "Six bucks each," he flatlines. *I don't appreciate not having my calls returned.*

There's that tidbit I didn't want to know about.

"Jordy." Camila gives a tight smile. "How about you let us in for free and I'll have coffee with you later?"

I roll my eyes.

As if Jordy is dumb enough to fall for that.

"You bet." He quickly opens the red velvet rope, and before I know it, Camila and I are on the other side.

She chuckles as we drift away from him.

"Works every time." She lifts a prideful shoulder my way. "Don't give me that look, Bizzy. I'm not going to stab his ego to death—just like I didn't stab Blair."

"That's still up for debate."

Something in the room catches my attention.

"Hold onto that thought," I say as I observe twice as many tables as there were yesterday. The dolls have all been moved to the right of the room with Annabeth safely back in her glass case and tucked in the middle of the haunted melee. And in through the side door, men in black with the words *Madame Tarantula's* written in orange across their chests hoist in new glass boxes and set them out on the spare tables.

Georgie and Juni are up front wearing matching witch's hats, and they seem to be directing traffic to this curio circus.

"Come on, Camila. I have a bit of business to tend to first."

We speed our way over, and to my horror the new glass cases are brimming with spiders of every shape and size, the biggest and hairiest of which is the size of my fist.

"What in the world?" I hold my breath to keep from screaming. "For the love of my sanity, Georgie, make it stop."

Georgie chuckles. "You're not the first person who's said that to me. Be original, would you?"

Juni snorts. "I've heard those words a time or two myself—mostly in the bedroom."

A groan springs from my throat. "Do not extrapolate. And what's with testing the limits of my arachnophobia? Are you kidding with the spiders? I really wish you would have opted for something a little less intimidating."

"Like guillotines?" Camila offers.

"I was thinking more along the line of quilts."

Georgie taps her chin with her finger. "For a newlywed, you really are a bit high-strung."

Camila's chest pumps with a dry laugh. "Maybe they haven't done the deed yet?"

Georgie holds up a finger. "This is Bizzy we're talking about. It's certainly not outside the realm of possibility."

Juni laughs like a fiend. "Some people wait until they get married. Maybe Bizzy here is waiting until she gets *buried*?"

Georgie gives a throaty laugh. "Straight to the freaky stuff. That's why I like you, Biz."

"All right, ladies." I take a moment to offer up my discontent. "What's really going on?"

"Spiders, Bizzy!" Georgie slaps her hands together with glee. "After that freak electrical storm yesterday, I got to thinking maybe the haunted dolls weren't my best idea yet.

But I'm going to make it up to you with these eight-legged wonders. And don't you worry. I've got a couple of taxidermy rats coming, too. Biggest the world has ever seen. Just wait until you feast your eyes on them."

"I can wait," I say.

Georgie gasps. "Oh, and before I forget—great news! Annabeth is back in her glass coffin and all is right with the world."

"I know she is." I lean in. "I was there when Jasper locked her inside." I quickly tell them about my bedroom misadventure and that nasty note. "If that doll is going to threaten me, the least she can do is spell my name right."

Camila shudders. "Creepy. I don't like dead bodies, and I don't like dead dolls."

Juni shakes her head. "Make no mistake about it, she's very much alive."

Georgie nods. "I can vouch for that."

"I'm afraid I can, too," I mutter, mostly to myself.

"And don't disparage her spelling skills." Georgie shakes her head. "Victorian Era dolls didn't have all the educational opportunities that the dolls of today have."

Camila nods. "Half of my dolls came with a computer chip in them."

Juni leans in. "I only went for the male dolls. Imagine my surprise when I discovered that the manufacturer lied on the box when they claimed they were anatomically correct. We should have sued, Mama."

Georgie nods. "The statute of limitations never closes for two things, murder and messing with my baby. Remind me to lawyer up once this gig is over."

"Anyway"—I take a breath as I attempt to pull us away from this sparkling conversation revolving around lawsuits and less than anatomical plastic body parts— "Jasper had a team come in and dust for prints. It turns out, the electrical storm the night of the murder knocked out the security cameras, so there was no help there. It seems whoever broke into my cottage walked right through the front door. I may have forgotten to lock it." But in my defense, Jasper and I have been enjoying some very late nights that leave little room for things like sleep or sanity.

And since the aforementioned activities took up most of the night, I never did get around to telling Jasper about the fact I've decided to reinsert myself into the case. What can I say? It's a woman's prerogative to change her mind.

Juni moans and inadvertently does her best impression of a ghost. "Annabeth strikes again!"

I shake my head. "I don't think Annabeth had anything to do with it." I glance to Camila. "More like the killer."

The three of them gasp so hard I'm half-afraid they've vacuumed up a spider into their lungs.

"And that's where you come in." I look directly at Camila. "Tell me everything you know about Blair and everything that went on that night."

She hitches her head to the mother-daughter duo in our midst.

Juni grunts, "Don't worry about us, sis. We're a part of Bizzy's dream team. We're the best and brightest."

Georgie nods. "She's the best and I'm the brightest."

Camila rolls her eyes. "Oh, for Pete's sake, I don't care who knows. Fine." She takes a breath as she looks my way. "I met Blair while I was in college. I was friends with Raven first, and she's the one that introduced me to Blair. Raven eventually decided she wanted to go to beauty school instead, but we still kept touch. And over the years, I met Sabrina and Tabitha."

I step in. "We're you very close to Blair?"

"Not really." Camila swallows hard as she gives a quick look around. "She was a little too uptight for me. Boarding school baby, wannabe socialite, the whole nine years. She was also a very successful realtor, which she often brought up whenever the four of us got together." She gives a sideways glance out at the haunted doll depository. "Anyway, last week, Tabitha called me out of the blue and asked if we could get together. She said she and the other girls were doing something new and she thought I might like it. When I agreed, she mentioned that they were all planning on meeting at the frightmare and asked if I would join them. When I heard it was here at the inn, I wasn't all that thrilled. I had planned on staying away from this place forever now that you and Jasper made it official." She takes a moment to frown my way. "But there I was again, right where I didn't want to be. That explains why I was in a sour mood that night."

Georgie twitches. "What's your excuse the rest of the time?"

Camila shoots her the stink eye before reverting her attention back my way.

"As I was saying, things got off on the wrong foot. It didn't help that Blair openly criticized my costume—and accused me of having an Electra complex." She wrinkles her nose. "She somehow deduced that me dressing like a young girl equaled me engaging in a psychosexual competition with my mother. Sabrina let me know that Blair was taking psychology classes at the local community college." She shrugs. "I guess that was her way of flexing her knowledge."

"And it made you angry?" I tip my head, trying hard to contain my disbelief.

"It was a good start." Her brows arch. "I asked Tabitha about that conversation we had the week before. I wanted to know what she meant by they were starting something new. A part of me wanted to speed things along. I planned on ditching out early. There was no way I wanted to run into you there—glowing and gloating about your honeymoon with the man who was supposed to be *my* husband."

I make a face. "Fine. That's how you felt. I can appreciate that. Go on. What led to the argument you had with Blair?"

"That's the thing. I didn't have an argument with Blair. She asked if we could talk and led me over toward the edge of the field."

I shake my head. "That night, after the murder when we were crowding around the scene of the crime—the woman dressed as a librarian, *Tabitha*—she said she heard you tell Blair that you had enough."

She makes a face. "I did say that. I said I had enough—enough of all the loud music, the screaming, the smell of carbs I was actively denying myself. But not anymore." Her lip twitches. "Let's just say I made quick work of those hand pies you brought over."

Georgie gives a dramatic snap of her fingers. "So she misunderstood you!"

"Exactly," Camila says. "I wasn't in the best mood, but I didn't snip at Blair either."

"So what happened when you got to the edge of the field?" I motion for her to speed it along.

"Nothing. We got there. I tossed my staff down over the hay because I was tired of holding it. Blair started to talk about some special society she was a part of. I think she was going to invite me to a party or who knows what?"

I tick my head to the side with suspicion. "Why separate you from the other girls to do that?"

"Who knows?" Camila shrugs. "Maybe she didn't want the others at this party? They weren't exactly getting along. Lots of bickering was going on about nothing in particular. I could sense the tension as soon as we were all together. Another reason I wanted to get out of Dodge."

Juni leans in. "So what happened out in the field? Did you bash her over the head with your staff?"

"No." Camila gives her a dirty look. "Blair started in about her society function and something caught her eye and she stopped cold. She told me to leave right away, that someone was coming and they would need privacy. And when I didn't budge, she shouted for me to leave. Believe me, I didn't need to be told twice, so I took off—without my staff." She glowers down at her feet a moment.

"Camila"—I whisper—"did you see who was coming to speak with Blair?"

"No, but I heard shouting almost immediately, and I just kept walking."

"Did it sound like a man or a woman?" I ask.

"It sounded like Blair. I didn't hear much from the other person, and I, unlike you, Bizzy Baker, am not a snoop."

I make a face. "Okay, Camila. Somebody stabbed Blair Bates that night. Who do you think did it?"

Her lips twist. "I can't be sure, but I did see something odd at the beginning of the night. Tabitha was yanking at Blair's arm, whispering something to her feverishly, and Blair was the one who looked fit to kill." She shudders. "I remember thinking something horrible was about to happen, and it turns out, I was right."

"Where can I find Tabitha?" I don't hesitate with the question. "Do you know where she works?"

Camila bats her lashes as she tries to recall. "At a seafood restaurant called Davy Jones' Revenge out in Whaler's Cove."

I nod. "Well then. If Tabitha is on tonight, it sounds as if I'm having seafood for dinner."

Georgie elbows Juni in the ribs. "Sounds like a stuffy place. Maybe we should bring Annabeth along to liven up our spirits. Get it? Spirits?"

"No way." I'm quick to put the kibosh on that haunted good time. "That doll isn't coming anywhere near me ever again."

The lights flicker on and off and an icy chill permeates the air around us.

"That's just a coincidence," I whisper.

But something tells me it's not.

7

It turns out, Tabitha Carter *is* working tonight.

And that's exactly why after helping Emmie with a few odd details concerning the frightmare that continues to terrorize the inn, Georgie, Juni, Camila, and I have ventured out to Whaler's Cove for a night of delicious Maine seafood and a side helping of suspects. Okay, so it's just the *one* suspect, but if all goes well, the killer will be served his or her just desserts.

Jasper said he's running a little late, but that he'd meet up with us as soon as he was able.

A part of me is dreading his arrival. Not only will the sight of Camila set off his suspicious antennae, but once he sees Tabitha floating around the place, he'll realize that vow I made back at the station was nothing more than a puff of dead air—lying dead air. But I didn't mean to lie.

Davey Jones' Revenge is a large brick building festooned with enough cobwebs, ghosts, and ghouls on the outside to convince the masses that it's every bit haunted for this late great month of October. But unless I see Annabeth inside noshing on crab cakes, flickering the lights the way she likes to do, I won't be at all convinced.

Leave it to Georgie to turn the Country Cottage Inn into a veritable haunted house. Of course, let's not forget Emmie's hand in it. I'll admit, I felt bad leaving her tonight, but I promised as soon as I got back I'd help out with the festivities. I won't lie, everything looks so cheerful during the day, with families coming out for hayrides, little ones running along the sand to pick out a happy orange globe to take home, and I've even run through the haunted maze set up out back with its walls made from hay bales—and I've enjoyed all of it, too. I made Jordy lead the way through that haunted maze, and held onto his belt loops with my eyes closed just to say I did it, and yet I still had fun.

But as soon as dusk hits, it's showtime, and the monsters come out in droves. I'm not a big fan of the spookier side of Halloween, and yet I've agreed to do the spookiest thing of all this scary season—chaining Camila Ryder to my side.

"Look at this place, Bizzy. It's good and snazzy." George sniffs.

Both Georgie and Juni have decked themselves out for a night on the town.

Georgie has donned her signature kaftan, in an apropos hue for this dark and pumpkin-shaped month, black with orange sequins.

Juni has on a black leather dress—short, with a squared-off neckline, and she's paired it with a pair of fishnets that have rhinestones running up the back of her legs.

Camila looks as if she was ripped out of a fashion catalog, with her full-bodied hair flowing in perfect form, and a crimson sweater dress that hugs her curves tighter than a racecar at the track.

And seeing that I knew Camila would be stepping up her game, thanks to the fact I'm allowing her the chance to have dinner with the ex-fiancé she's still more than mildly obsessed with, I've stepped up my game, too. I pulled out my crimson sweater dress and thigh-high suede boots with heels.

Okay, Camila and I are basically wearing the exact same thing. It seems I crawled a little too deep into the Camila Ryder-inspired end of my wardrobe. A massive misstep that I won't let happen again. The next time we plan a little outing like this, I'm demanding she sends me a picture of the stitches she's chosen to outfit herself with. God forbid people think we're playing twinsies on purpose. It's bad enough she wants to play twinsies with my marital status—with my *husband* if you want to get right down to it.

We step inside the establishment, and the sound of loud rock music vibrates right through to our bones. The scent of chowder and French fries infiltrates our senses, and seeing that there's about an hour wait, we put our names in and head for the bar.

It's dimly lit inside, the floors, walls, and furniture are all made of dark wood, and there's a nautical theme running throughout. The bar is about as spacious as the dining room, and there are even people dancing in the middle of it. But unlike the main dining room, the bar is furnished with high tables that you can easily set your drinks down on, at a standing height. Lucky for us, we manage to snag one close to the bartender with tall stools set around it.

"I can't sit in these." Georgie pushes her seat away and opts to stand. "I've got vertigo. I'll fall over."

"Don't fall over," Camila commands. "The last thing I want is for us to end up in the ER because you cracked your head open like a piñata."

Juni snickers. "I bet candy would fall out—Red Hots to be exact."

Camila snorts. "I bet nothing would fall out."

"Watch it, sister," Georgie huffs. "Or there will be a fallout, all right. It just so happens that my friend Bizzy Baker *Wilder*"—she winks my way when she says my newly minted moniker—"can pin a homicide on whoever she wants. And if she wants to send you up the river for the next fifty years, it's hasta la bye-bye to ya. So you'd better be nice to me. Those are the rules. Pick a fight. I dare you."

"Now that we've established the rules of fight club," Juni slaps her hands down over the table, "let's cut to the coital chase. How many men apiece are we looking at?" She cranes her head as she asks the asinine question.

Camila shakes her head my way. "What's happening here?"

"Just a typical night out for the three of us," I say without batting a lash, because let's face it, it's true. "No limit on men," I tell Juni. "But you're both leaving with me. Collect all the numbers you want, leave the STDs at the door."

Georgie and Juni emit a sharp whoop.

"You heard the lady." Georgie elbows her baby girl. "Let's get cookin'." She leans in. "Bizzy, order up some appetizers. I'll head to the bar and pick up a few tasty treats."

"Oh, that won't be necessary," I say. "I see a waitress headed this way."

"I'm not going for drinks, hon." She gives a little wink before knocking her head toward Juni. "Come on, chica. Let's make a game of it. First person to score seven digits is buying tonight."

Juni's eyes round out as she leans toward her mother. "I thought you said Jasper was buying?" she hisses as they make their way to the bar.

Camila shoots me a look that can slit my throat. "Again, why did they have to tag along?"

"Because if they didn't, we'd look like a couple of matching sister-wives on a date with our husband."

Her eyes sweep up and down my body. "You do have good taste in both fashion and men." Something by the door catches her eye and she gasps.

"Is she here?" I glance back and gasp right along with her.

"No, it's your hot brother and that ditz of a mayor he's leashed himself with."

Before I can laugh or agree with her—on that part about the ditz of a mayor, not the hot brother part, although in all fairness I've been told Hux is a looker—the two of them are upon us.

"Well, well." Mackenzie Woods sizes the two of us up with wide eyes. Mackenzie is the current mayor of Cider Cove. She's followed in her father's footsteps and her grandfather's before that. A part of me thinks the good people of our cozy town voted for her because they were used to having a Mayor Woods in office. There's comfort in repetition—and a serpent named Mackenzie, too. "If it isn't the Bobbsey Twins. Is it red dress night? I didn't get the memo." She shakes her head. ***Out on the town with the hussy looking to score a home run with her husband? I will never understand Bizzy Baker.***

Some days I don't understand myself. This is definitely one of them.

Both Mack and Hux are dressed to the nines, with her in a little black dress and him in a suit and tie that brings out the I-make-bad-decisions look in his eyes.

Mackenzie Woods is definitely the bad decision in question.

"Bizzy?" Hux ticks his head to the side as he pulls me in for a hug. "Playing with the piranhas tonight?" he whispers in my ear.

"I could say the same for you." I give him a little wink.

He pulls back and makes a face. ***Can't wait until she finds out I'm thinking of proposing soon.***

"*No!*" The word rips from me with horror, and soon all eyes are feasted this way. "Um"—I clear my throat—"I mean no, don't tell me the two of you have to endure an hour wait for a table, too."

"Geez." Hux inches back, and don't think I don't notice how easily his arm glides around Mackenzie's waist as if he were protecting her from me. And he just might have to. Don't get me wrong. I'm just starting to make peace with Mackenzie after all these years of torment, but she'd be the last candidate I'd choose to spend the rest of her life with my brother.

Mackenzie rolls her eyes. "No, Bizzy. Unlike you and your new girlfriend, Hux and I made reservations. We just finished up with our meals and were about to leave when he spotted the two twits he thought he recognized." She makes a face at my brother and mouths the word *sorry.*

"Oh?" My shoulders hike with a touch of glee. "Well, that's too bad because I would have offered for you to join us." It's true. I'm a glutton for punishment that way.

Mackenzie gargles out a laugh. "And spoil this romantic rendezvous? We couldn't." ***We wouldn't.*** "Where does that new husband of yours fit into the equation, anyway?" ***Bizzy is up to something. She's no pushover when it comes to the good detective. I should know, I tried to wrangle him away from her for old time's sake.***

Mackenzie was pretty darn good at wrangling away anyone with an extra proverbial limb away from me back in high school. She recently claimed she was testing them out to see if they would cheat, and sadly just about every single one of them took her up on her offer—save for Jasper, of course.

Camila sniffs her way. "My husband will be here shortly."

"She meant *my* husband," I quip.

Mackenzie shakes her head. *Why Bizzy does what she does, I will never be able to wrap my head around. There's no way I'd entertain the sluts Hux has been with—and funny enough, I'm pretty sure Camila Ryder is one of them.*

Camila smacks me on the arm. *Get rid of them. Tabitha just spotted me and she's headed this way.*

I gasp as I survey the area, but I can't seem to see her. It might just be a ploy of Camila's to get rid of the scourge before us, but it happens to be a scheme I'm willing to go along with.

"Don't worry, Bizzy." Mack sneers. "I don't have to be a mind reader to know you want us out of your hair. Hot tip, the lobster is to die for." She shrugs my way. "Maybe you can work that into your next homicide somehow? Oh, and by the way, tell Georgie I fast-tracked the approval to let her display those quilts."

"What quilts?" I lean my ear her way, because if this is another one of Georgie's questionable initiatives that involves the inn, I want to be in the know—or more to the point, I want to know if I need to line up one exorcist or two.

Mackenzie gives a long blink. "The Cider Cove quilting guild donated dozens upon dozens of those dusty pieced together blankets to the town over fifty years ago, and they've been in storage ever since. Apparently, Georgie found out there was an entire slew of them inspired by fall and

Halloween, and she said she wanted to display them at the inn."

"Well, now that sounds perfect." I breathe a sigh of relief.

Mack shrugs. "She said you were the one that requested it."

I rewind the last few conversations I've had with Georgie, and by Georgie, I think she's right. Sort of. I said I'd prefer quilts to spiders, and I stand by my statement.

The two of them say goodnight and take off just as Tabitha Carter appears at our table. Her hair is up in a bun, and she's dressed like a vampy little vampire this evening. Gone are the librarian glasses, replaced with a cherry red smile as she yelps and gives Camila a spontaneous hug.

"What in the world are you doing here?" She smacks her friend on the shoulder.

Camila's lips twitch. "My friend Bizzy invited me out to dinner."

Tabitha grimaces as she looks to the two of us. *Her friend Bizzy? I would swear on my life Camila said she couldn't stand the woman's guts just a couple of nights ago. I guess some people will tolerate just about anyone for a free meal—and my guess is, Bizzy is buying.*

I shoot Camila a look, and she frowns as if she understood what just transpired.

She clears her throat as she looks to the friendly vampire among us.

"We're—um—discussing a business proposal I have for the inn. I'm keeping it short. Bizzy is actually having dinner with friends."

How I hope that's true.

Camila nods and shakes her head all at once, and it's a dizzying look to witness.

"I was actually about to pitch Raven's products like she asked," Camila continues. "And now that you're here, you can vouch for how wonderful they are."

"Raven?" I say her name with a touch of intrigue. "The girl with the long hair I met the other night?" I refrain from calling it the night of the murder.

"Yes." Camila nods. "That's the one. Not only does she run her own hair salon, Color Me Crazy, but she has a perfumery."

Tabitha offers a feverish nod. "She has a home lab where she creates her own scents. Don't worry. It's sanitary—your ears won't fall off or anything. Raven's been cooking up lotions and potions for as long as I can remember. And believe me when I tell you, her perfume can cast a proverbial spell on anyone you've set your sights on."

Camila looks my way. "She calls them Sultry Scents. She has a few generic bottles, but mostly she specializes in creating a one-of-a-kind scent for you and your paramour."

Tabitha leans in and her excitement is palpable. "First, she asks questions about you and then the guy you're looking to snag. And once she gets a profile of the two of you, she creates a scent guaranteed to land your man. It worked for me." She gives a quick look around. "I had my eye on one of my supervisors for months. The man is seriously hot. And well, after having Raven concoct the perfect perfume, I was able to claim him." *Just for a night. It turns out, the louse has a girlfriend. And how I hate that I inadvertently became the other woman. Not only that, but sleeping with him has all but guaranteed I'll never move up in the ranks around here. Raven's potions are more or less cursed. Just about every relationship she's brought together with those ridiculous Sultry Scents has ended in tragedy. Lord knows Blair and Dr. Feel Good weren't exactly what you would call a horseshoe.*

Dr. Feel Good? I blink at the name. I could swear I heard Blair mention him the night she died.

I nod as if I was smitten with the smelly idea. "Sounds great. In fact, I'd love to have Raven come by. Maybe she can set up a booth at the Fall-oween Festival? I know that Sabrina will be giving tips on face painting soon. I'll see if I can work something out where they're together."

"That's great." Tabitha's face lights up with gratitude before her features darken a notch. *Hey? Now that Blair is gone, maybe I can be the one to bring both Camila and Bizzy into the Maidens? I was the one inviting Camila to begin with, but as soon as Blair met Bizzy, she insisted on giving her to Sabrina. I'm not sure what that move was about. Everyone knows the rules. You find your own noble downline. And right now, I'm declaring these two are mine.*

What in the heck is a Maiden? And *downline*? Why does that term sound familiar?

"I'm glad things worked out for you," I say.

Tabitha gives Camila a sideways glance. *Too bad they didn't work so well for Camila. I can't believe she told Raven that she wanted her money back after the love of her life married someone else. Although it was a bit comical when she said she'd pay twice as much as Raven was asking if she'd cook up some genuine poison in the cauldron of hers. It sounds as if Camila really has it out for whoever it is who stole her fiancé.*

I look to Camila and roll my eyes.

"So Tabitha—" Camila must be able to read minds, too, because she is wisely getting down to brass tacks. "What's going on with the girls? How are you all handling this? I know you were all a lot closer to Blair than I was."

"Not on the night of the murder." Tabitha gives a sly wink. "Kidding. I know you didn't take her out." She turns her head away for a moment, and that seemingly innocent move makes me wonder about her own innocence. "We miss her." She shrugs as if she were truly indifferent.

Of course, I don't miss her personally, Tabitha muses to herself. *That wily witch can rot in Hell for all I care.*

Then again, perhaps she's not so indifferent.

"Were you and Blair close?" I nod over to her as I ask the question. I already know she didn't like her. Now to squeeze the reason *why* out of her brain.

"We used to be." A far-off look appears in her eyes as if she were reliving better times. "But life, you know, got in the way. She was a very important person. Blair was a realtor, and that kept her busy. And she was taking night classes at the local community college."

"Oh?" I lean in. Camila already told me so much, but I want to see if that road leads anywhere before I abandon it. "Was she trying to earn her degree?" Maybe she didn't finish when she went to school with Camila way back when? I went to college and didn't finish, but only because I was afraid of actually succeeding at something. A horrible and long story that I've long since pushed out of my mind.

Tabitha squints to the ceiling. "You know, she never mentioned that. I think she was just taking it for kicks." She shrugs. "Like I said, Blair wasn't exactly forthcoming with the details of her life those last few months, not to me anyway. But we were still very connected." *The Maidens guaranteed that. Speaking of which...* "I should probably take your orders and get back to my tables, but how about the three of us get together sometime? I'd love to continue the conversation. And Bizzy, I can tell right away that you and I are going to be great friends."

My mouth falls open. "I can tell the same thing," I say. "Name the time and place. I'll be there." With investigative bells on.

"Great." Her eyes widen. *Wow, that was easier than I thought. I can't believe I have two live ones— and they're mine all mine.* "It's sort of a mixer I'm a part of. It's actually my turn to host."

"Ooh." Camila wiggles her shoulders. "I don't think I've ever been to your place."

"Sorry." She cringes. "It's not at my place." *Like I'd ever want to show anyone the hovel I'm living in. I'd have to instruct the Maidens to bring Tasers and mace just to walk to the door.* "I'm still looking for a venue, but as soon as I have the details I'll text you." She nods to Camila. "And if you don't mind sharing it with Bizzy, I'd appreciate that."

"Done," Camila chirps.

A thought comes to me. "If you need a venue to host your party, the inn has tons of rooms. I'm sure I could accommodate your needs. What kind of a party is it?"

Wouldn't she like to know. Tabitha offers a slight wink my way. "I'd like to keep it under wraps for now. It's sort of a surprise."

Great. I hate surprises, Camila muses.

Me too.

Tabitha's brows meet in the middle as she considers my offer. "Yeah, maybe I'll touch base with you. We'll see. Can I get you ladies any appetizers? The witch's fingers, pumpkin dip, and mummy baked Brie are super popular."

"We'll take all three," I say. Not only am I starving, but I have a feeling Georgie and Juni are going to need something solid in their stomachs sooner than later. I see them both at the bar, sipping on something purple with a matching colored fog billowing out of their glasses, while hitting on every man that's breathing—and maybe some that aren't. "Tabitha, can I ask you a question? Was there anyone there that night who had an axe to grind with Blair?"

Camila grunts, "Yeah, who do you think she was chewing out after I left her?"

Tabitha's lips knot up. **I had it out with Blair, but I'm not about to say it. Especially not since Camila made a big stink about how Bizzy here has solved every homicide in Maine for the last year solid. She** *also mentioned she was the one doing the slaughtering and cleverly setting people up, but still.*

Tabitha had it out with Blair? Was she the one Blair was arguing with right after Camila left? My word, is she the killer? And leave it to Camila to out me—ironically, it's not serving her well.

"Raven." Tabitha nods my way. "She and Blair were on the outs regarding the society."

"What society?" I ask without missing a beat.

Tabitha brings her fingers to her lips a moment.

"I meant to say our society. You know leftwing-rightwing views. The two of them have never seen eye to eye politically. Anyway, I'll get your order in." She takes off and Camila and I exchange a glance.

"What's this society?" I ask. "And does the word *maiden* ring any bells to you?"

Her mouth falls open. "Is that what she was thinking about?"

I loathe the thought of outing myself officially to Camila as far as my supernatural abilities go.

"Maybe," I say. "So what does it mean?"

"I don't know. But the last thing Blair mentioned to me was something about a society function. Maybe this is the same thing?"

"I guess the party goes on," I say. "But that word *maiden.*" I shake my head. "I'm getting the feeling it's some sort of guild or club. I'll have to look it up."

"Don't worry, Bizzy. I'll look it up, too. Believe me, I'm rolling my sleeves up, and I'll be getting dirty right alongside you. I want the spotlight off of me and my good name cleared."

I choose not to comment on the state of her questionably good name.

"So what do you know about this Raven chick?" I ask. "I met her, but it was brief."

"Raven is the real deal. A good friend through and through. And she's always been loyal to Blair."

"Why do I get the feeling Blair was the queen bee?"

"Because she was. And believe me, I hated seeing Raven bowing down to her the way she did. I guess things soured between them, but Raven Marsh is no killer."

"I'll talk to Raven and see where I can get. Hopefully, she'll tell me all I need to know about the Maidens, and who knows? Maybe she did kill Blair, maybe she didn't, but here's hoping that a little chitchat with Raven will end this investigation for good."

Camila lifts a brow. "You mean the chitchat I'm about to have right along with the two of you. Believe me, I'll be able to pull all the dirty little details from her, no problem. Are you free tomorrow?"

"I can be. What are you thinking?"

"I'm off early. I'll book us both an appointment at her salon. Once she sees we've dropped some serious dough, she'll be good and primed to spill all she knows. Raven and I always share a cup of coffee together afterwards, right there in the salon."

"A kaffeeklatsch in hopes to catch a killer, can't wait."

"Who's going to catch a killer?" a deep voice rumbles from behind, and every muscle in my scheming body freezes. I recognize both that voice and that heady cologne already ensconcing me in its warmth.

Juni and Georgie run over.

"Jasper is here, six o'clock!" Georgie points behind me.

Juni lifts her foaming purple concoction our way as if she was toasting us. "Glad to see we didn't miss the show. Let the fireworks begin."

Camila filled both Georgie and Juni in on the fact that I swore to Jasper that I'd stay out of the case. The three of them seemed to have a good laugh on my behalf on the drive over regarding it, too.

"Bizzy?" Jasper steps my way, and I quickly wrap my arms around him and offer up a smothering kiss that comes with promises and maybe a slight bribe that suggests we hold off having the inevitable conversation until we're alone.

Jasper Wilder is a vision tonight in his dark suit with that equally dark look in his eyes as his brows hover over those pale gray peepers like a couple of birds in flight.

"Ladies," he offers an amicable nod to the trio of women, "what's going on, Bizzy? Why is Camila here?"

Apparently, my new legal plus one isn't the mind reader I was hoping he'd be.

Camila's chest vibrates as she struggles to swallow down that chortle stuck in her throat.

"I was just about to take off," she says. "But if there are going to be fireworks, who am I to miss the show?"

Jasper offers me a stern look. "Why would there be fireworks?"

I take a deep breath. "Camila asked me to help get her off the hook and I agreed." My stomach cinches. "I meant to tell you when you got off work last night, but well, Annabeth had other plans." And so did we.

Jasper groans, and I'm not sure if it has to do with Annabeth or me—probably both.

"No fireworks." He dots a kiss to my cheek and looks tenderly into my eyes. "I figured a U-turn was inevitable, albeit I'll admit you still managed to catch me off guard."

"Stick a fork in me." Camila rolls her eyes. "Turns out, I'm not sticking around for the show after all. Have a nice dinner." She looks my way. "We'll talk."

She takes off just as my name is called over the speakers, letting us know our table is ready.

Georgie lands an arm over Jasper's shoulders. "Good thing you're here. We just lost our ride."

Juni nods. "And we might need you to spot us for dinner."

His lips curl as he looks my way. "It's good to know I come in handy once in a while."

"How about coming in handy tonight for me?" I tease, and both Georgie and Juni whoop and holler. "At the frightmare." I shake my head as I correct them. "I'm dying to take a hayride. Rumor has it, it's haunted."

Jasper chuckles. "I take it Annabeth's the driver?"

"Let's hope not," I say. "But just in case, we'd better stock up on garlic and holy water on the way home."

We enjoy a fancy meal composed of delicious Maine lobster while I tell Jasper all about my exchange with Tabitha.

"She might just be the killer," I whisper.

"She might be." His chest widens with his next breath.

"Why do I get the feeling you're not telling me something?"

His eyes close a moment too long. "Forensics found cell samples under Blair's fingernails."

"Do you know who they belonged to?"

He gives a curt nod. "We already had her DNA on file. They belonged to Camila."

8

The frightmare is well underway when we arrive back home, and the Country Cottage Inn is fully transformed once again into the haunted house it never wanted to be.

Thankfully, the inn itself is off-limits for the participants of this scare fest. And for that reason alone, I've decided to close down the haunted doll—and spider exhibit each night at seven. There's just too much going on, too many people, too many monsters on the loose for me to keep track of.

I asked Jasper if I could question Camila regarding how her DNA might have gotten under Blair's nails, and he said I could have at her. He said normally he'd want to haul the suspect in and record the event for analysis of their facial expressions, but he assured me Camila was a pro when it came to keeping a poker face.

So I sent her a text and laid it out for her, but she hasn't replied yet. Needless to say, I'm not too interested in seeing her poker face either. I figure she could lie to me just as easily over the phone as she could in person—or tell the truth for that matter. As for reading her mind, that feels like sort of a moot point with Camila. She's onto my mind-reading ways whether I want to admit it or not.

Jasper shakes his head as he looks to the crowd around us as we walk the haunted midway. The stars shine above Cider Cove despite the intricate network of twinkle lights, and it all adds an enchanted appeal.

"You'd think after a human being was killed here the other night everyone would want to steer clear of this place," he says.

"And yet the crowd has doubled in size," I point out. "Sadly, I think that grisly murder is the sole reason for it."

The haunting mood music is a touch too loud for me, with its creaking doors, the ceaseless screaming, the faux thunder, ominous footsteps—all under the backdrop of rather dramatic organ music. But apparently, they're deep-frying a fresh batch of apple fritters not too far from where we're standing and the scent of vanilla and sugared up apples more than makes up for the spooky ruckus.

"Rumor has it, that haunted hayride is pretty good," Jasper teases as he lands a kiss to the back of my hand.

"Too bad we won't find out for another twenty minutes." We bought our tickets as soon as we arrived but missed the last hayride by seconds. "How should we kill the time? You want to win me a stuffed pumpkin? Or take a bite out of one of those caramel apples with me?"

"I've got something else I'd rather take a bite out of," he says, whisking us to the dark area just past the haunted maze.

Jasper wraps his arms around my waist and lands a searing kiss to my lips.

"Why do I get the feeling you've pulled this move before at a haunted festival or two?" I ask.

"That might be true. But just for the record, I've been polishing my moves for my bride. That would be you, in case you forgot."

"*Ohh.*" I wink. "I did forget. Care to remind me?" I hook my arms around his neck, and just as I go in for a kiss, my phone chirps. I pull it out. "It's Camila. She said she's sorry she missed my text. She was in the shower. And as far as her DNA being under Blair's fingernails, she says she tripped when they were on their way to those hay bales where Blair met her demise. She says she was about to fall when Blair tried to intervene and Blair ended up scratching her on the arm instead."

Jasper lets out a breath as he thinks about it. "Okay. Fine. I'll jot that down in my official notes. I'll have to question her again regardless. But I don't want to think about Camila now." He dots a kiss to my nose, then each of my cheeks before landing another on my lips. And just as we're about to launch into something we can both sink our teeth into, the sound of a chainsaw ramping up from behind sends me screaming as I clutch to Jasper for dear life.

The madman wielding the chainsaw runs our way wearing a hockey mask and looking every bit the terror he's attempting to be.

My voice shrills as I hop onto Jasper as if he were a pole, and the next thing I know, he's carrying me.

The maniac takes off to terrorize a group of girls, and we watch as they scatter like birds in his presence.

Jasper's chest vibrates with a laugh, and I can't help but frown up at him.

"Oh, so you think this is funny?" I ask while poking him in the chest. "I may never sleep again." Although at the moment that has more to do with whoever broke into my house and planted a haunted doll on my bed, but that's not the point.

"It's not funny." He squeezes his eyes shut, the laughter still caught in this throat. "Okay, it's a little funny. You do realize this is all fake, right?"

"That's exactly what I was saying about those haunted dolls right up until all the power along coastal Maine was knocked out for hours. I'm telling you, something wicked is in the wind, and it's in the ballroom at the inn, too."

"It's been twenty minutes. Let's go see if there's anything wicked on that haunted hayride."

Jasper whisks us off in that direction and, to our surprise, we find Georgie and Juni in line to board the haunted ride as well. They've both donned capes of some sort and look ready to scare up some screams with the best of them.

Soon, we're all loaded onto the back of a flatbed, hitched to a trailer, furnished with hay bales that create a cushy yet prickly place to sit—with Juni, Georgie, Jasper, and me situating ourselves on the end.

"Guess what, Bizzy?" Georgie plucks something out from the cloak she has draped around her, and before I know it, that haunted porcelain doll that's embedded her way into my nightmares is thrust in my face.

A viral scream rips from me, and then soon enough just about everyone unfortunate enough to be on this haunted ride is screaming right along with me as the giant doll glows in that pale muslin dress she's wearing.

"Why in the heck did you bring her along?" My voice is still shrill with both surprise and a touch of anger.

"She looked lonely." Georgie gets right to cradling the pint-sized terror. "Besides, I wanted to be the one to break the news to her."

Juni butts her shoulder to her psychotic mother. "What news is that?"

Georgie makes a face. "I've broken down and conceded to Bizzy's demands. I've got a bunch of fall-themed quilts coming to the ballroom tomorrow because Bizzy wants to give the little orphan girls the boot."

I shoot a quick look to Jasper and shake my head before reverting to Georgie.

"If the haunted dolls mean that much to you, Georgie, go ahead and keep them until the end of the month. I would never ask you to remove them. But I won't lie, I think the quilts are going to be a welcome relief."

"You mean it?" Georgie looks thrilled to have the heresy continue.

"Yup," I say. "Just keep Annabeth away from me. No offense, but she is a little creepy."

Georgie scowls my way. "Don't listen to her, Annabeth." She pets the doll's stiff red curls. "Bizzy was a little creepy kid herself. I've just never wanted to hurt her feelings and say it out loud."

"Yeah." Juni sneers my way. "And not only that, but now that she's an adult, she hates kids."

About three different mothers look my way.

"I don't hate kids," I'm quick to assure them. "I plan on having a few myself." I shrug up at Jasper.

I say we get home and practice. He waggles his brows.

"Something tells me our night should have started and ended there," I whisper.

The tractor makes an abrupt stop and Annabeth goes flying into the air, sending just about everyone stuck on this contraption screaming in terror. Jasper reaches up and snatches her to safety before she accidentally falls onto someone and cracks their head open—most likely mine.

"Give her to me," I say, lackluster, as if acquiescing to the inevitable. "I'll hold onto her extra tight and make sure she doesn't wreak anymore havoc." I settle her onto my lap for the remainder of the journey, and not shockingly, nothing is nearly as scary on this adventure as she is. The ride comes to a conclusion, and we disembark with the rest of the passengers.

"How was that for a romantic ride filled with a few chills thrown in for good measure?" I ask, rattling Annabeth in Jasper's direction.

Juni shakes Georgie by the shoulders. "Check out the hot guy in the hockey mask."

Georgie cranes her neck. "The one holding the chainsaw?"

"That's him." Juni links arms with her mother. "You know what that means?"

"He's going to chop up our bodies and make a stew out of us?"

I think Georgie has it right.

"*No*," Juni wails. "It means he's employed. And believe me, I've dated a gardener or two before. They really know how to use their hands."

They take off in hot pursuit of the masked man, and as soon as he sees them coming, he turns and darts the other way.

Smart gardener.

"Wait a minute," I shout up over the music and noise. "Georgie! You forgot Annabeth!"

Jasper slips his arm around my waist. "Something tells me they knew exactly what they were doing."

"I guess we should take her back to the exhibit, but that's the last thing I want to do. I'm ready for bed."

"I like how you think. Let's leave the doll in the living room."

"Fish, Sherlock, and Sprinkles may never forgive us," I say.

"We'll take our chances."

We head for home, and I groan as we head down the cobbled walkway that leads to our cottage.

"Why does it sound as if that frightmare is taking place directly in our backyard?" I tease.

"Because it is." Jasper gives my ribs a tweak. "Now let's get to bed. I vote tomorrow night we start there to begin with. I'll bring takeout."

"Ooh, a picnic underneath the sheets? I'm in. Hey, maybe we can watch a movie?"

"Or we can find another way to entertain ourselves."

"I like how you think." I laugh, but Jasper doesn't join me on the endeavor. Instead, his expression grows hard as he stares straight ahead.

"What in the heck is that?" He flashes his phone over the front door, and in red lipstick against the crisp white paint it reads, *You didn't listen. You're next.*

I jerk back at the sign, causing Annabeth's head to swivel around until she's looking right at me, and she gives a solid wink.

A killer, a haunted doll, and a stalker.

How could this month possibly get any worse?

9

"I want to tell Emmie tonight," Leo Granger says the words with a marked conviction as we stand just outside of the Country Cottage Café.

Tonight? Fish groans in my arms. *You've waited all these years to tell Emmie your secret. Surely there must have been less hectic moments in your life to do so. I think I'm going to veto this idea.*

Leo chuckles as he gives her a quick scratch on the head.

"Think about it, Bizzy," he says, and those dark eyes of his plead with mine.

I take in a full breath as I look to the ocean then to the clouds up above which look dark and looming. It's icy out with a biting wind. The Atlantic churns with anger. The unknowable deep is the color of the darkest sapphire this afternoon. The sand is heavily gouged as dozens of happy children and their caretakers prance around inspecting all of the orange globes dotting the vicinity. And as Leo and I speak, another batch of pumpkins is being unloaded onto the sand. Just beyond that, I spot Emmie standing under the reception tent where the register is housed.

There's a long table in front of the counter filled with exotic gourds in every shape and size, and Georgie is there plucking her way through them. But it's Emmie I focus in on, that cheerful smile of hers as she goes around from customer to customer offering up the jack-o'-lantern hand pies from the platter she's holding. She's dressed in a red cape and looks every bit the adorable Little Red Riding Hood.

"Why tonight?" I look back to Leo with a sigh while Sprinkles and Sherlock run loose underfoot. I'm holding Fish close to my chest, and she's warming me right through my peacoat. "I mean, the Fall-oween Festival is going strong. And we've got the frightmare starting a little earlier in the evening tonight. People are loving it, they're demanding more hours. Emmie is really the one running this show. Don't you think she's overwhelmed enough as it is?"

Sherlock runs up and barks. ***Bacon, Bizzy!***

I don't hesitate reaching into the little baggie in my hand and tossing both him and Sprinkles a few bits of the savory treat. I figured this was the only way to keep them from running up and down the cove. There are so many people here—so many small children. All of which would love to pull their tails and ears while trying to love them to death. Not that I could blame the kids—Sherlock and Sprinkles are both exceptionally cute.

"Bizzy"—Leo glances her way—"Emmie was just telling me that the Montgomerys' staff is filling in all the blanks around here. They're running the festival, top to bottom. She and Jordy wanted in on the action so they could monitor things for you, for the inn. And"—he winces as looks back my way—"I know that it's you who's overwhelmed. You came back from your honeymoon to this circus, not to mention there was another murder on the grounds. And now that you're questioning suspects, the killer is onto you. I saw the note they left in your bedroom, and the lipstick on your door this morning. Where did you sleep last night?"

"At home," I say.

Fish shudders in my arms. *And I hated it. I didn't feel safe, not even with Jasper and his weapon, or Sherlock and Sprinkles snuggled on either side of me. I had to sleep with one eye open. I hope the sun comes out today, because a nap in the sun is certainly in order.*

A tiny laugh brews in me, but the situation is so dire that laugh doesn't make it past my throat.

"Jasper had a few deputies stationed outside on night watch," I tell him. "And he's enlisted round-the-clock protection. He has three different security teams here installing new cameras. He already changed the lock to the cottage the other day, and he's having a whole new alarm system installed this afternoon. I guess the wires were frayed in the last one. And as for the lipstick, it's being washed off as we speak."

"Lipstick." Leo lifts his belt a notch. "Do you think the killer is a woman?"

"Maybe. But it could be a man trying to throw me off."

Fish burrows her head against my chest. *I hate killers.*

Sprinkles runs up and lets out a sharp bark. *I'm going to help find whoever did this, Bizzy. If I can be of any help at all, I'm willing to do it. Just say the word* bacon, *and I'll give you a hand.*

"Thank you," I tell him. "I'm going to take you up on that." I toss out a few more pieces of bacon to prove my point.

Leo tucks a smile in the corner of his cheek. "I'd ask how the killer knew about your super sleuthing skills, but Cider Cove is a small town. Word gets around. And the word about you has certainly gotten around. Be careful, Bizzy. Jasper has told me more than once he's worried about you." The wind picks up, and he tightens his coat around his body.

Leo is clad in his deputy uniform, tan shirt and pants with a black wool coat on top. He looks handsome enough, and every now and again I see Emmie sneaking glances his way. She's probably wondering why we're gabbing out here and not headed in her direction to say hello.

Leo nods. "She is wondering just that."

"So you can read her mind so easily?" I muse. I'm not exactly sure how easy it is for Leo to read anyone's mind, but it seems unfair that he can single out her thoughts at such a distance.

"I can," he says with a touch of sadness. "For some reason, I can pick up on Emmie from twice this far. I guess we're just that in tune."

"Correction," I say. "*You're* just that in tune."

A dull chuckle streams from him. "How about dinner tonight? The four of us. We can tell her then."

"Too formal. Besides, she won't be able to eat, or digest properly after we fill her in on a whole new level of terror."

"Okay, how about we do a little bonfire out on the sand?" he counters. "I'll bring the blankets, the chairs, all the makings for s'mores. We'll bring our pets, you bring yours. We'll have fun. The four of us—we're practically a family, Bizzy. And families shouldn't hold secrets like this."

Sherlock Bones and Sprinkles bark and whimper all at once.

Sherlock barks the loudest. ***Oh please, Bizzy! Can we? Jasper always gives me a bite of his hot dogs at a bonfire, and I know he'll do the same for***

123

Sprinkles. And Cinnamon and Gatsby will be there. They have to meet Sprinkles.

Great. More dogs. Fish groans and closes her eyes, doing her best to take a nap. *I'd ask to be left home alone, but I can't chance that doll showing up again. Don't have children, Bizzy. Their toys are terrifying.*

I look over to Emmie and watch as she shares a warm laugh with Georgie—Georgie who already knows my secret. But Emmie isn't Georgie. She's going to be disappointed in me for withholding something so big for so long. She'll be terrified of me. And speaking of terrifying things, I can't help but notice that Georgie is right back to schlepping around that haunted doll. She's hoisted her onto her hip as if she were a toddler, and she's picking up gourds and showing them to Annabeth as if she expects the doll to talk back to her. And knowing that doll, she just might.

"How about this," I say as I meet up with Leo's dark eyes once again. "Yes to the bonfire. But as far as telling Emmie about our telesensual abilities, we play it by ear. If it feels right, we go with it. If it feels forced, we pull back and try again some other time. It's going to happen, Leo. I already know that. But the last thing I want is for this to go sideways."

A knot builds in my stomach because at the moment I don't foresee another direction.

"Sounds perfect." His entire countenance lights up. "It won't go sideways, I promise." He pulls me in for a quick embrace. "We'll see you at the cove at seven. How does that sound?"

"Like a whole new frightmare." I'm only partially teasing.

"I need to take off, but I'll let Emmie know about the bonfire. I'll make sure things go smoothly between the two of you, Bizzy. I'm not looking to wreck your friendship."

He takes off, and I decide to give him a minute before I head that way myself.

"Things are going to go sideways," I say as I plant a kiss on Fish's furry head. "Doesn't he recognize a pattern when he sees one? This whole month is going sideways."

Fish stretches her paws high up over my chest and mewls. *You don't think the killer will strike again, do you?*

Sherlock barks. *Fish is only asking because she's afraid she'll be next. Don't worry, Fish. I won't let that happen.*

Sprinkles barks and dances in a circle. *If the killer did get anywhere near us, I'd bite their ankles.*

"You're a little sweetheart," I say, picking up the tiny darling. "Guess what? I'm headed out to speak to Raven today. I'll ask to see if any of her friends are interested in adopting you." Jasper said he spoke to Blair's parents, both of which live out of state—and separate states at that. Neither of them was interested. And Blair had no siblings, so there's that. "Do you like any of her friends?"

Sprinkles whimpers. *Not in particular. They were always so gruff with one another. And I've seen them point fingers at Blair when she turned her back.*

I'm guessing it was a specific finger they were pointing. I get the feeling not a lot of people got along with Blair.

A thought hits me. "Hey, Sprinkles? Did Blair ever mention anyone named Dr. Feel Good around you?" If the killer is a man, I'm afraid he's my only viable suspect in that arena.

Dr. Feel Good? she chirps. *Oh yes. Blair mentioned him all the time. She was forever asking me if Dr. Feel Good would love this dress or that. Or which shoes she should wear to meet up with him. She talked about him incessantly to the point of nausea. It was too much of a focus on one person. Her time would have been better spent focusing on me.*

"I agree with you there." A tiny laugh escapes me. "Sprinkles, do you know his real name? Or can you describe him to me?" That man in the tan trench coat comes to mind—the one I bumped into as soon as I stepped into the inn the night of the murder. The same man I saw shaking

Blair then slipping cash into her hands—the same cash that was scattered all around her when I found her body as well. I distinctly remember he had a dark beard and commanding light eyes. If Sprinkles describes Dr. Feel Good that way, I'll know exactly who to look for—sort of.

Never saw the man, she yips. *And I'm sorry, Bizzy, but I don't remember her calling him by any other name.*

"No need to apologize," I say, watching as Leo takes off with a wave, and I wave back. Another thought hits me. "How about the word *maiden*? Have you ever heard her mention that?"

She gives a soft bark. *Oh yes, I've heard her mention the Maidens plenty of times. The Midnight Maidens this—the Midnight Maidens that. It was happening all the time.*

I suck in a quick breath. "The Midnight Maidens?" Those words Blair spoke the night she died suddenly make sense. She said just because we have *midnight* in our name, doesn't mean we need to *start* at midnight. Huh. I guess that's one mystery solved. But it bloomed right into another. "Sprinkles, do you know what the Midnight Maidens were about? Something to do with her real estate ventures maybe? A club?"

She whimpers. *I'm afraid I can't recall much more than that. She was always saying how she had a love-hate relationship with them. She called them her witches. And how I wish I would have paid better attention beyond that.*

"Not to worry. But if you think of anything else, let me know."

Her witches? Could this be a cult of some sort? Leave it to Camila to embroil herself in a coven and not even realize it.

I head down to the sand as I make my way over to Emmie and Georgie standing side by side while looking at the gourd collection. They come in every shape and size, and I'll be honest, a few of them are downright vulgar looking.

"Hey, Bizzy"—Georgie holds up an elongated yellow gourd my way—"what does this remind you of?"

I squint down at it before making a face. "*Georgie.* There are kids around."

"No, not that." Georgie rocks Annabeth on her hip. "It looks like a banana. But I can't fault you for having your mind in the gutter. You're still technically on your honeymoon. I have a cousin who's French, and she took two years away from the world just to do nothing more than lie in bed with her new hubby."

"*Ooh,*" Emmie muses as she takes Sprinkles from me. "A two-year honeymoon sounds perfect. It sounds like I should start saving up." She winks my way. "And before you ask, no, he didn't propose. But I can sense it, Bizzy. What was he talking to you about for so long?" She bats her long lashes my way. "I just know he's up to something. I can feel it."

I can feel it, too.

I force a smile. "You're right, he's up to something. A bonfire at the cove tonight."

"Oh, goodie." Georgie gives Annabeth a jostle. "Hear that, kiddo?" She gives the haunted doll another shake. "We'll be roasting weenies by the fire tonight." She nods my way. "What's on the agenda this afternoon, kid? I've got a new pick-up line, and I'm dying to use it."

"Let's hear it," I say. I might as well work it out of her system.

"Hey, big boy"—Georgie's head swivels as she winks—"is that a gourd in your pocket, or are you just glad to see me?"

"I don't know, Georgie." Emmie shakes her head. "That might be too much firepower."

Georgie shoots her a look. "At my age, sweetie, you need all the firepower you can get. But most importantly, he's got to be able to fire back. No point in shooting my ammo at him if he can't even hold up his weapon."

"I'm meeting up with Camila," I say, choosing not to get tangled in the trenches of that conversation. "We're getting our hair done at noon."

Emmie lifts a brow. "You never get your hair done. I'm guessing you're on the hunt for a suspect again."

"You bet I am. You want in?"

She's back to making a face. "If Camila wasn't there, it would be a fast yes. But since she's in the equation, it's a hard no. I'm just sorry you have to be there yourself."

"No problem. Hey, would you mind keeping an eye on Fish and Sherlock? I've got a crew installing a new security system. Jordy's overseeing it, and I plan on taking Sprinkles with me."

"It would be my pleasure," she says, trading Sprinkles for Fish. "I'll have Cinnamon come out. They'll have a blast."

Georgie stretches her arm to the sky. "Count me in. I haven't had my hair done since 1953. And I bet Annabeth has got a good fifty years on me in that department. We're just two old girls living with old curls."

"And old curses," I muse as I look to the haunted doll. "All right. Meet me in the lobby at eleven forty-five." I give Sprinkles a quick kiss to the nose. "We've got a killer to catch."

10

The Color Me Crazy Salon is set right in downtown Seaview, a hop and a skip from the sheriff's station, which would explain why Camila beat me here.

By the time Sprinkles and I arrive—with Georgie and Juni in tow—Camila is standing in the entry talking to a familiar brunette with half her face done up to look like a skeleton. It's a convincing look on her, too, as it should be. Sabrina Ames is an expert at wielding a makeup brush.

Camila is wrapped in a rich brown cashmere sweater, and Sabrina looks every bit the makeup artist rock star she is in a black leather jacket and dark ripped jeans.

"Sabrina," I practically sing her name, thrilled to somehow have procured a two-for-one suspect sighting. I give Camila a slight wave, and she flexes a short-lived smile right back.

"Hey, Bizzy." Sabrina pats Sprinkles on the head. "Hey there, girl. I hear Bizzy is taking really good care of you." She smiles my way. "I was just asking Camila about her, and she mentioned you still had her."

I nod. "And I'm loving her, too. I guess Blair's parents can't take her. If either you or your friends are interested, please let me know. If not, I don't mind keeping her."

Juni hops over on one foot. "I'll call dibs if this baby girl has nowhere left to go. I've got a spot on my bed that could use a tiny cutie to warm it."

"Thanks, Juni," I say. "I'll let you know."

Sabrina makes a face. "Sorry, Sprinkles. I'm a cat person, but by the sound of it someone will scoop you up." She looks my way. "I'm sure it's getting tight in that tiny cottage with three pets." *Although with the drop-dead gorgeous husband like that—who would care? I'd sleep in a closet as long as he was with me.*

"It is." I laugh. "But we like to think of it as cozy."

Sabrina glances to her phone. "I'd better go. You ladies have fun. I just had time for a blowout this morning. I'm doing a makeup tutorial at the local high school. And don't think I've forgotten about the tutorial I'm doing at the inn this week. Camila let me know you're going to ask Raven to join us. It's going to be a blast."

She gives a friendly wave as she takes off, and I take a moment to soak in the crazy salon that's living up to its kooky moniker. The floors are a dizzying black and white checkered pattern, as bright red chairs and turquoise framed mirrors dot every station.

There's an array of women in every sort of costume, ranging from zombies to princesses, exerting a touch of sass in their choice accouterments as they hum over their clients, working busily to make sure they leave with just the right look. And the entire place holds the scent of lemons and ammonia.

Cobwebs and white muslin ghosts are strung up in every corner, and a giant black cauldron sits on the reception desk filled to the brim with candy. There's a miniature Snicker's bar peeking out at me, and I make a mental note to snag it before we leave.

"Great news!" Georgie hops over from the reception desk with that silly yet scary doll bobbing in her arms. "They've got room for two more, Juni. I'm thinking big hair. What do you think?"

Juni snorts. "Go big or go home. We're going to have to hit the clubs tonight, Mama, just to show off our new dos."

Georgie moans. "Don't you tempt me. You know I've got this little monster to mind. I can't go unless I find someone to sit on her." Her eyes bug out as she hooks her gaze to mine. "What do you say, Bizzy? I've watched Fish and Sherlock plenty for you. How about a little tit for my tat?"

Camila groans. "Oh good Lord, just say yes, Bizzy, so we can get on with it."

"Yes," I hear myself says as Georgie and Juni whoop it up.

"You won't regret this," Georgie says and immediately her expression sobers up. "But whatever you do, don't get her wet or feed her after midnight."

Thankfully, the receptionist leads the mother-daughter duo to the back, and Camila motions for me to follow her.

"Sounds like I've got a Gremlin on my hands."

Camila shakes her head. "Georgie and Juni are both Gremlins. Not the good kind either. The kind that were dunked in water and fed greasy tacos far past their bedtime. That doll is the least of your worries."

"You haven't met that doll," I quip as I give poor Sprinkles a squeeze.

Raven Marsh waits in the back with an ear-to-ear grin as she scoops Sprinkles right out of my arms and begins to kiss her furry little face. No sooner does the smooching commence than the sneezing starts.

"Hey, ladies." She sneezes again. Raven's jet-black hair drapes over her body like a cardigan. She's wearing a skintight orange dress and a pair of black leather boots that stretch to her thighs. Painted under each of her eyes there's a harlequin pattern, and her smile is painted well past her lip line, giving her all the appeal of a sultry clown. I'm guessing that's Sabrina's genius at work.

"Take her," she says as she hands Sprinkles back to me. "I've got mean allergies to pet dander. No luck in placing her somewhere, huh?"

"It looks like I may have a home for her after all," I say, glancing in Juni's direction. "But I'll check around with the rest of Blair's friends before I take that step."

Raven's eyes widen a moment. *Good luck finding people who identify as Blair's friends. The odds are better of finding a unicorn first. And the way this crazy month is going, she just might do that. Nothing would surprise me anymore.*

Nothing would surprise me anymore either. And I would definitely keep the unicorn. Our cottage may be tight, but there's always room for unicorns.

Raven looks to Camila and me. "You know what? I think I'm going to take care of the both of you at once."

She gets us to the back and washes our hair before landing us in those red shiny seats right back at her station.

Camila nods my way. "So, Raven"—she says as the blow dryer hums on a low setting above her—"we ran into Tabitha last night at dinner, and she mentioned those perfumes you're cooking up. I'm betting if I had gotten my mitts on them last year, I'd be Mrs. Jasper Wilder instead of you, Bizzy."

I avert my eyes as Raven cackles up a storm. I know for a fact she did try them because I read Tabitha's mind back at the restaurant the other night. Let's just say these perfumes don't have such a great track record.

"It's amazing you're friends at all." Raven ticks her head to the side. *Come to think of it, Camila didn't have a single nice thing to say about Bizzy the day we met. Typical Camila. Smile to your face, stab you in the back when you're not looking.*

A quick visual of Blair lying on the ground that night bounces through her mind and she gives a hard blink, shooing the thought away.

"Camila and I are past all that now," I say. "Isn't that right, Camila?" I do my best to give her a threatening look that says agree or die. Or more to the point, this *investigation* dies. Once the killer smells a grudge between us, this friendship act we're selling will be about as believable as Georgie's new baby. Although in Annabeth's defense, she's got some serious haunted street cred.

"That's right." A sickly smile wavers over Camila's face. "Bizzy and I are fast friends. She comes down to the station all the time with baked goods for Jasper. Of course, I'm his gatekeeper, so she has to get past me first." She winks my way.

Not a bad performance. Although, I'll have to tell her to never call herself my husband's gatekeeper again.

Sprinkles squirms in my arms. *Ask her about that night, Bizzy. Raven was always around. If anyone knows something, it's her.*

I give Sprinkles back a quick scratch to acknowledge her.

"Raven"—I say as she trots over to my chair and begins combing out my hair—"you have to tell me about your perfumes. What's your business called?"

"The Potion Perfumery." She shrugs. "I thought it sounded cute, a little mystical. And my perfume line is called Sultry Scents. I don't know if Tabitha mentioned it, but I put a lot of work into crafting the perfect aroma. Let's just say, women have used it to snag the man of their dreams, and the success rate is through the roof. I've garnered a bit of a reputation that way. A good one. Believe me when I say, business has been brisk." *Not to mention those Maiden meetings score me an easy couple hundred dollars each time we meet up. If anyone is ripe for a pipe dream in a bottle, it's those women.*

My mouth falls open.

Raven knows about the Midnight Maidens. Of course, she does. This is perfect.

"Please tell me you'll come to the Fall-oween Festival and do a little roadshow," I say as she smooths out my hair with her hands. "Sabrina will be there next week doing a tutorial. I can set you both up at a booth. I know for a fact you'll make a killing off my sister alone." It's true. Macy does love snagging herself a man, or twelve, and is willing to go to whatever lengths to do it. Shelling out a few hundred bucks for a potion is right up her alley.

"Are you kidding? I'd love to. Give me the details when you get them, and I'll be happy to show." *So they were with Tabitha. Makes sense. She's in need of a couple of girls. Here's hoping she's landed these two. Tabby isn't the most successful Maiden—and if the Maidens are going to move on like they should, that girl needs to step up her game.*

Camila snaps her fingers midair. "I almost forgot to mention. Tabitha invited us to some party she's throwing. She mentioned you'd be there, too."

Hey? If I didn't know better, I'd *really* think Camila was a mind reader. This isn't her first well-timed contribution to a conversation.

My eyes widen as I look her way.

You're not a mind reader, are you? I ask and she gives a quick wink my way.

Let's hope that was just a coincidence.

Raven clucks her tongue. "That is so wonderful! Will you both be coming to the party?"

"Oh yes," I say. "Tabitha mentioned the event had a name, the Midnight *Mavens*?" I shake my head and wait for Raven to correct me, but instead her eyes spring wide.

Typical Tabitha. Screwing it up from the get-go. She's supposed to wait until they arrive to do the big reveal.

"Midnight Maidens?" Camila's expression sours as if she was trying her hardest to give the answer to a pop quiz. *I just put that together, Bizzy. I bet that's what it's called.* She offers a smug grin my way, rather proud of her deductive logic skills.

Sprinkles moans. *I told you that earlier.*

I nod down at the cute pooch.

"Yup," Raven says as she pulls and tugs at my tresses. "Midnight Maidens. Did she mention anything else about it?" *Not that I would be surprised. Some people go through life with the directions wrong, and then they wonder how their life got so screwed up to begin with.*

"Nothing," I say. "Care to share the details?" I ask. "I'm super curious about it."

"Good." A smile of satisfaction crests Raven's face. "Let's keep the details out of it until the party. I promise it's going to blow your mind." *Let's hope it blows their wallets, too.*

Wallets?

Camila huffs, and the look of frustration on her face is evident. One thing is for sure, Camila Ryder can't hide her feelings.

"Raven?" She tips her head this way. "How are you holding up?"

Raven's shoulders sag a moment. "As well as can be." *More like as well as my acting skills will allow. Less Blair equals less headaches and more money. She was never good at sharing. But she was excellent at stealing.*

Wow.

"I miss her, too." Camila shrugs. "So that night, she kept talking about some mystery man. Who is Dr. Feel Good, anyway? Were they serious? I mean, I was thinking about it, and the fact she finally found love only compounds this tragedy."

"Dr. Feel Good." Raven rolls her eyes. "More like Dr. *No* Good. Believe me, Blair didn't find love. She found lust. And I'm pretty sure that's all she was interested in anyway." *Billy. What a jerk. I'm shocked the sheriff's department hasn't arrested him yet. From an outsider's perspective, I would think it would be obvious. But then, he is a professor. I doubt murder is in his wheelhouse. If his wife ever found out about the affair, she might be the number one suspect. But, from what Sabrina said, she's still in England visiting her mother.*

My mouth rounds out at the revelation.

"Oh, Bizzy," Raven coos down at me. "I'm not hurting you, am I?"

"Not in the least. In fact, you're helping—me relax. I'm sorry about your friend." I nod. "I mean it, I know this can't be an easy time for you."

"You got that right." She scowls while tugging at my tresses. *It's not an easy time because Blair made me empty out my bank account in order to keep that real estate office of hers up and running. She just had to keep up pretenses. I wonder what the Maidens would think of her if they knew she hasn't had a single sale in nearly a year—that she was having a hard time coming up with the rent for her home and her office. And now look who's out of all that money? Me. But I'm not a monster. If Blair would have paid me back, none of this would have happened. But—one of the last things she told me was that I would get my money back over her dead body. Ironically, little did she know that dead body of hers would show up sooner than later. And I still don't have my money. Oh well, I guess you can't have everything.*

Blair borrowed money from Raven? And refused to pay her back?

Winner, winner, motive dinner!

Raven works feverishly over Camila and me, and before we know it, we're both sporting bouffant hairstyles that have been teased and sprayed into a frozen flashback of the eighties. Scratch that. This is definitely circa 1960 something.

When all is said and done, we ante up and collect Georgie and Juni as we head outside.

I scowl over at Camila and point to the cotton candy heap on my head. "Why do I get the feeling Raven doesn't like you?"

"She loves me," Camila is quick to correct. "It's just her Southern influence at play, that's all. Everything is better when it's bigger. It says so right there on the sign."

I turn around, and sure enough, there it is in faded gold, hard to read cursive font. Go figure. I was walking into this spun sugar disaster and didn't even know it.

Georgie bucks with a laugh as she and Juni sport identical dos.

"Well, we love it." Georgie pulls Annabeth close to her ear. "What's that? Annabeth loves it, too!" She cackles once again before smacking her daughter on the arm. "We'd better get gussied up for tonight. The early bird dinner down at Lenny's is a hot spot I've been dying to hit." She hands Annabeth to me, and poor Sprinkles cowers as she struggles to scooch away from the haunted doll.

Raven didn't let Sprinkles get out of there free as a bird. She plopped a tiny pink bow into her hair for good measure and teased up the tresses just above her eyes. It's clear Sprinkles got the better end of the deal.

"I'll ride home with Juni," Georgie shouts as they take off down the street. "Make sure you buckle Annabeth up. She's very fragile!"

"Just like my sanity," I mutter.

Camila frowns my way. "So what's next, Detective Wilder?"

"Aw, you said my name and you didn't have one mean thought," I tease.

"I'm saving them all for later."

"At least you're honest," I say. "Next up? I think we should talk to Sabrina a little bit more."

"Okay, that should be easy enough. Hey, what about Raven? Did you read her mind? Did you learn anything new?" Her eyes strain as she leans in, as if she was trying to look into my brain for info as well.

"I don't know. Did *you* read her mind?"

She grunts as she looks skyward. "Stop with the stupid games, Bizzy. If I could read minds, I wouldn't need you. Now tell me what she said."

"Okay, if I *were* to read minds, I may have heard that Dr. Feel Good's real name is Billy. And the louse is married. His wife is in England right now. And if that's true, that rules her out as a suspect. She did hint that Sabrina knew him, too. Oh, and Raven may have mentioned something about Blair being good at stealing. It almost sounded like an inside joke, though." I shrug. "Of course, those are just things I'm guessing she would be thinking about. Nothing official."

Camila is back to rolling her eyes. "Okay, it sounds good. Billy..." She glances around as if she might find him lying on the floor. "I'll mention his name to Sabrina as if I knew him, and I bet she'll say something—or think it."

"Good. I think we're actually making strides."

"We had better be. My neck is on the line." She starts to take off. "Call me. I want this buttoned up soon."

"So do I." The less time I need to spend with Camila the better. Although, if I had to admit it, she's not all that bad to hang out with.

I shoot Annabeth a look. "You ready to head back to Cider Cove, kiddo?"

I waste no time as I strap her in the back seat as Georgie suggested, and for a second it feels as if I'm taking care of my own child, the child Jasper and I will have one day. My heart swells with joy just thinking about it.

A mother. I shake my head.

I could be a mother. I don't see why not. Jasper and I are in the perfect place in our lives. We could afford it. I could probably bring the baby to work with me. And my mother could pinch-hit. I'm sure she'd love to babysit. I know Jasper would be a great father. And look, I'm taking great care of Annabeth. I'd make a *great* mother.

I press my weight into it as I secure the buckle over her lap, and the sound of thunder crackling overhead fills the car right before her head falls off.

"*GAH!*" I scream while poor Sprinkles barks up a riot.

On second thought, maybe I'd better put a little more thought into this whole motherhood thing.

I drive back to Cider Cove with my headless toddler in the back and garner more than a few looks because of it. But I don't care. There's no shame in my haunted doll game.

The only thing I care about right now is tracking down Blair Bates' killer.

And I think I'm just a few steps away from making another head roll, straight for prison.

11

"Big hair don't care?" My sister, Macy, snickers as we stand just outside of the Country Cottage Inn.

It's dark out earlier than usual tonight. It seems that October's magic isn't just relegated to a harvest moon or two, but it has the capability to cut the day in half with an early nightfall as well. Not that I'm complaining. The more time I get to spend with Jasper, snuggled up next to a fire, the better, and in a way we'll be doing just that tonight.

"Very funny," I say as the revelry from the Fall-oween Festival blooms around us. That moody creepy music streams through the air as men, women, and children alike surge through the grounds.

The frightmare attraction doesn't begin for another few hours, so there are still plenty of little kids enjoying the games and rides set out in the meadow.

"So what brings you to this haunted neck of the woods?" I ask Macy while cinching a headless Annabeth onto my hip. I've got her head in hand and was headed to see Jordy about reattaching it somehow. If anyone can restore this haunted apex where it belongs, it's him. I would have done it earlier, but we had a rush of tourists all clamoring for a room.

I nod her way. "What gives? Are you here to add to your collection of stuffed teddy bears and unicorns? We've only got stuffed vampires and ghosts to choose from, but I bet they'll keep you warm on a cool autumn night."

"Now look who's the comedian?" She cinches a short-lived smile on her face. "Actually, I'm here to find something much more creative in keeping me warm at night." Her brows lift a notch as she takes in the crowd to our left. "A real vampire. I've heard stories about the way they entertain themselves well into the night, and I want to see firsthand if they're true." *This wouldn't be my first go-around with a neck biter. And I seem well able to attract them in and out of this haunted season. Mostly because I'm lucky.*

"Try a werewolf. With all that fur, at least you'll be warm." I join her in craning my neck out at the crowd as the twinkle lights strung up above illuminate the area. A man entering the gates to the meadow has me doing a double take and I gasp. "On second thought, never mind the werewolf. I see a man in a trench coat I'm far more interested in."

I start to take off and she pulls me back.

"Bizzy Baker Wilder, you are a married woman. The man in the trench coat is mine." *Especially since half the men I've dated in trench coats had nothing on underneath.*

"No way," I hiss as I rattle Annabeth's head at her and she takes a full step back. "The man in the trench coat is a suspect who I happen to know very little about. If I can get close enough, I might actually be able to hear what he's thinking."

She balks, "And how would you do that? Are you a mind reader now?"

A breath hitches in my throat. With all the light, sounds, screams, thrills, and chills, not to mention Annabeth's decapitated head in my hand, I've momentarily forgotten that my spicy sister has no clue about my ability to pry into other people's headspace.

"More like read his face," I say as I speed in that direction, and soon both Macy and I are walking through the midway, but it seems the man in the trench coat—who just might be this mysterious Billy the unhappily married professor—has done a disappearing act. "Shoot, we lost him. I guess my trench coat radar is off."

"Mine isn't." She swats me blindly as if to garner my attention at whatever she's looking at and gasps as she smacks Annabeth's head in my hand instead. "That thing just bit me!" Macy brings her hand up, and sure enough, a thin seam of blood erupts over her finger.

"How about that," I muse. "It looks as if I've got a biter on my hands." Or in them, as it were. "Sorry, Mace. But could you blame the girl? You did smack her on the head."

"Because I was trying to get your attention." She cranes her neck once again. "I see him! He's headed toward the edge of the field. He's got something in his hands."

I jump up in an effort to see over the crowd, and there he is headed toward the left end of the meadow that's still cordoned off.

The Montgomerys thought it would be in bad taste to reopen the area where Blair Bates was slain, so the caution tape is still up and Jordy put in a temporary barrier of chicken wire fencing just outside of the caution tape in hopes to stave off the lookie-loos. Nonetheless, mobs of people magnetize in that direction each and every night, and some have been tossing bouquets of flowers and the stuffed animals they've won at the game booths onto the spot where she was slain.

"He's holding flowers," Macy grunts.

We head in that direction ourselves but stop shy of entering the sparsely populated clearing. There he is, in the same tan trench coat as he walks that way with a surefooted gait. A woman stands near the impromptu memorial, and it looks as if he's meeting up with her, or exchanging a few words in the least.

"Drats," Macy hisses. "Looks as if someone beat me to him."

"Never mind him. You're here for the vampires, remember? Not potential killers."

The woman turns our way, and I get a clear shot of her front side. She has dark hair and is wearing some sort of a skimpy costume, but it's those heavily decorated arms that glow green and blue even in this dim light that alert me to who she might be.

"I think I know that girl," I say as we edge in just a bit closer. "I think it's Sabrina Ames, a makeup artist. The very next suspect on my list, in fact. *Huh*. I guess she does know him. And I think he was the deceased's boyfriend."

"*Ooh*"—Macy squeals—"he's newly grieving. Let me at him."

My phone buzzes in my pocket, and I pluck it out. It's a text from Emmie.

At the cove! Jasper and Leo got home early. They brought takeout. I've got Fish, Sherlock, and Sprinkles along with my furry crew. Saving a seat for you.

"I gotta go. I'll be at the cove if you need me. Have at any man here except that one."

"You know me. I obey orders." She gives a sly wink. "And by the way, Bizzy, motherhood is a good look on you. Word to the wise, I wouldn't let Jasper see the headless doll. He might rethink that whole parenthood thing."

"You're probably right. Don't do anything goofy. This month is already off on the wrong foot."

"What else could possibly go wrong?" she teases, but she doesn't take her eyes off of the man in the trench coat, and now I know exactly what could go wrong.

I take off, and soon enough I'm on the other side of the property, walking down the sand toward the friendly bonfire illuminating the night at the far end of the cove.

It's quiet for the most part out here, a decent distance from the revelry at the pumpkin patch, and I see Emmie and Leo holding hands as they sit by the fire while he stokes the flames and our furry menagerie runs wild along the shoreline. The briny scent of the ocean paired with the fresh flames warms me from the inside out. There's nothing better than an autumn bonfire on the beach with thick wool blankets and cups of hot cider.

Bizzy! Sherlock barks as he heads my way. ***They're here! They're here! Cinnamon and Gatsby!***

Sprinkles runs up looking like nothing more than an adorable furry little house slipper in comparison to the lumbering beasts around her.

Hello, Bizzy! she chirps. *I got my feet wet! Fish says my tail will fall off if I head into the water. Is that true?*

I laugh and shake my head, just as both Cinnamon and Gatsby run up and I offer them a quick scratch on the head. Cinnamon looks every bit the labradoodle teddy bear she is, and the color of her coat lives up to her name. Gatsby is a golden retriever with long flowing hair and glowing amber eyes.

Cinnamon gives a friendly bark. *Leo brought Emmie a bouquet of bacon.*

Gatsby howls. *It must be true love.*

Sherlock does his best to vocalize. *The best part is— she's sharing!*

That's my bestie. Emmie has a heart of gold. She would do anything for anyone, especially for me. Our friendship means the world to her—as it does to me.

My heart drums as I come upon the three of them. I can't bear the fact that tonight just might be the very last night of what I was hoping would be a lifelong friendship. And thanks to Leo's incessant need to bring Emmie up to supernatural speed, it might just end tonight.

"Bizzy?" Leo stands. **Not true.** He offers a friendly smile.

"Here she is." Jasper swoops over and wraps his arms around me. "Kiss me."

"Anything for you." I offer up a smooch that lets him know this is just the beginning of what I'm hoping will be a very long night.

My beautiful bride. Your hair looks great.

"My hair looks like a glob of cotton candy was dropped onto my head. But I like your ability to see past the obvious when it comes to my follicular mishap."

Fish gives a quick yowl. *I'm warming your seat for you! The canine crew is running into the water. I tried to stop them, but apparently they don't care if their tails fall off.*

A dull laugh rumbles from me.

"Hey, Biz," Emmie says as I take a seat between her and Jasper. "What's that in your hand?" Her face contorts as she struggles to make sense of it.

"It's just Annabeth," I say as Fish jumps in and out of my lap with a hiss.

"*Gah!*" Emmie inches back. "Why?" She looks adorable wrapped in an oversized flannel, which I'm guessing belongs to Leo, and a black and white silk scarf hanging loosely around her neck.

"I'm babysitting for Georgie."

"That makes total sense." Jasper groans. "We've got Chinese. How about we set Annabeth on this blanket down here? That way you can enjoy your meal."

"Sounds good." I hand her off, and soon we're all diving into the take-out boxes as if we've never seen food before. And right after we empty those out, Emmie breaks out a platter of her scrumptious jack-o'-lantern hand pies and we each partake in the yummy pumpkin goodness.

"So wonderful." I moan. "I'd ask for the recipe, but I think we both know that would be futile." Despite being born a Baker, my surname did nothing to ensure that I'd be a wonder in the kitchen. I'm more of a one woman walking disaster—burning, singeing, and incinerating as I go. Jasper has kindly offered to help keep the two of us alive by way of takeout and pizza from here to kingdom come. It's not the healthiest diet, but we're always eating something delicious.

Emmie shakes her head. "You have the gift of hospitality, Bizzy. I have the gift of baking. How about I take care of dessert for the next fifty years and you host all of our parties?"

"Done deal," I say before turning to Jasper. "So how's the case going?"

"Big news." His silver eyes flash my way. "I wanted to tell you in person." He nods to Emmie and Leo. "Don't say anything, but it turns out, Blair Bates was six weeks pregnant."

Both Emmie and I gasp at the very same time, and if I'm not mistaken, I think I heard Annabeth gasp, too. Fish is seated in front of the porcelain monster with a look in her eye that suggests she's ready to pounce.

"Jasper," I say. "I bet it belonged to that married professor she was seeing." A thought hits me. "I bet that's why he was giving her the money the night she died. He was trying to get her out of his life."

He leans in. "Bizzy, do you know the name of the man with the tan trench coat?"

"Billy. Or at least I think it is."

Emmie clucks her tongue. "Bizzy, you're amazing. I'm sorry, Jasper, but this girl is dancing circles around the Seaview Sheriff's Department."

Leo chuckles. "That she is."

Jasper twitches his brows. "Don't I know it. We've talked about it." A slight look of defeat crosses his face and I feel terrible.

Leo clears his throat. "How about we change the subject to something a little lighter?" *Are you ready, Bizzy?* He ticks his head my way and I gird myself.

Just like this Leo? I didn't even get the chance to run it past Jasper.

Leo lifts a brow. *I had a feeling you wouldn't, so I did run it past him. He knows and he says as long as you're fine with it, he is, too.*

Emmie squints my way then does the same to Leo. "What's going on? Why are the two of you looking at one another like that? You've been awful secretive lately. You're not having an affair already, are you, Bizzy?"

"And we're sideways," I mutter to myself. "Not now, not ever," I say, taking up Jasper's hand and giving it a hard squeeze.

"Actually" —Leo's chest widens with his next breath— "there is something I wanted to—"

"Bizzy!" my name wails from somewhere down the beach and the dogs go wild barking and running.

Fish's ears perk as she darts in that direction just as Georgie and Juni come trotting this way.

"It's Georgie!" A slight rise of panic hits me. "Quick, give me the doll," I say and Jasper hands her over in two pieces. "Oh no, I forgot all about her head. I'm about to get busted. Anyone have any glue in their pockets?" I glance to Em and that pale piece of silk glowing around her neck. "*Ooh*, your scarf, Emmie, quick." I flick my fingers at her, and soon enough, I've secured Annabeth's head right back onto her body."

"There she is." Georgie takes Annabeth from me. "I hope Auntie Bizzy has been treating you well. What's that? She let you have at the Halloween candy?" A hard groan emits from her. "Great. Thanks a lot, Biz. Now I'll be up all night scraping this one off the ceiling. You know what candy does to a kid."

Juni chuckles. "We just had a couple of handfuls of candy corn for dinner ourselves."

I can tell, but I don't say a word. Georgie's been having a fistful of candy corn for breakfast for years now, claiming it's for medicinal purposes, of course.

Leo nods. "You know, if there was a Halloween candy food pyramid, candy corn would be a vegetable. I think you did pretty good all things considering."

Juni grunts, "Good thing I saved room for dessert." She lunges for Emmie's jack-o'-lantern hand pies, and both she and Georgie load up on them. "We'd better get going. I've got a hot date that involves my television set, a roaring fire, and a pair of fuzzy socks."

"No luck at the club, huh?" I ask.

Juni makes a face. "How do you think I got the hot date? There's a man with a pointed tail and horns coming over in five minutes. Here's hoping he likes hand pies."

Georgie nods. "I hope my date will like them, too. I've got a mummy swinging by in half an hour. He said he might be late because he's all tied up." She laughs like a madwoman. "Get it? *All tied up?*" She gives a hard wink. "Here's hoping he's not the only one tied up this evening." She glances down at Annabeth. "Thanks for watching the kid, Bizzy. Here's your scarf back." She gives it a quick tug, much to the protest of those of us seated around the fire, and we watch in horror as Annabeth's head goes flying and lands smack into the center of the flames.

Emmie and I shrill out a quick scream. Georgie and Juni howl as if someone just knocked their own heads right off their bases. And Leo and Jasper hop up, trying to fish that head out of the inferno before us as if it was filled with cold, hard cash.

Leo jabs at it with a stick while Jasper pulls his foot back before kicking Annabeth's head right out of the fire. We watch in amazement as the doll's head flies through the night sky like a comet with its tail on fire, only to put itself out in the sand.

It's a wild end to a wild day.

Georgie and Juni collect what's theirs—or more to the point, what's Annabeth's, and take off for the night.

The four of us wrap up our bonfire and do the same. Both Leo and I agreed there was too much going on for us to share the supernatural news with Emmie tonight. He suggests we try again in the very near future.

Jasper and I make our way back to our cottage with our furry counterparts and we head straight for bed.

Although, we don't get much sleeping done. Just the way I like it.

And tomorrow, I plan on hunting down Sabrina Ames and asking a few questions about dear old Billy boy. I can't wait to get to the bottom of Blair Bates' haunted homicide investigation.

And I have a feeling I'm about to do just that.

12

Last night when we got back to the cottage, I told Jasper all about seeing Billy and Sabrina out by the makeshift memorial.

Although I'm not too sure he heard. Jasper had other things on his mind, and well, lucky for me, not one of them involved a homicide case.

It's the very next morning and I've already sent Camila a text. I gave her a bit of homework and told her to track down Sabrina's whereabouts today. I mentioned we could use the fact she's going to be doing a Halloween makeup tutorial at the inn as a cover if we have to. But it's pertinent to the case we speak with her as soon as possible.

After checking in a steady stream of guests into the inn, I leave the registration counter in my co-workers' capable hands and take Fish, Sherlock, and Sprinkles to the ballroom with me.

No sooner do I walk into the palatial space than I see the configuration of the room transformed once again. The dolls and spider displays have taken up the right side of the room, but it's the left side of the room that's getting all the action—and by action, I mean the masses have turned out to witness this new cozy display.

Quilts of every size and color are laid out over dozens and dozens of tables. Each one looks more intricate than the next, and almost all of them have adhered to a strict color palette of purple, green, black, white, orange, yellow, and brown. There are magical looking quilts with nightscapes, lots of black cats and full moons, witches, ghosts, skeletons, and enough autumn leaves to furnish all of Maine.

Fish purrs in my arms. ***Oh, I like this, Bizzy. Can we pick up a few of these for the cottage? I especially like the one with all of the black cats sitting in tiny squares. I've been thinking we need more of a feline presence in the cottage now that the canines have moved in.***

No matter how many times I seem to explain to her that Jasper isn't a canine, she keeps referencing him as so.

"That's a good idea," I whisper. I'd much rather bring home a blanket with twelve cats on it than twelve cats. "But I don't think they're for sale."

Sherlock and Sprinkles take off as they make the rounds, and the entire room is instantly smitten with them.

"Bizzy!" my mother calls out from the front of the room, and I see that she's got my spicy sister by her side. I can't wait to see what Macy found out about Billy last night, if anything.

"Hey, ladies." I pop up next to them, and they both give Fish a quick scratch. "Isn't this amazing?"

Mom lets out a groan. "So much better than those haunted dolls and spiders. I'm still having eight-legged nightmares. You know, just last night I had a nightmare that one of the doll's heads fell off and was pitched into a fire. Can you imagine that?"

I give a hard blink.

Should I be worried that Annabeth's reality has crawled into my mother's dreamscape?

Fish shudders. *I don't like this, Bizzy. Those dolls don't belong here. We'll have to take a blowtorch to the place just to cleanse it once they leave.*

She's not kidding.

Mom looks cozy for fall in her bright orange sweater with the stiff white collar from her blouse popping up from underneath. The eighties may be long gone, but Mom holds firm to the preppy spirit it sponsored. And Macy looks dressed for success in her tight, orange and pink knit dress, paired with adorable slouchy boots in the perfect shade of merlot. I've always envied my sister's fashion sense, especially since raiding her closet is a heck of a lot harder now that we no longer live together.

"Sorry about the nightmares," I wince.

Macy makes a face at my mother. "I told you not to look them in the eyes."

"Never mind that." Mom waves her off. "I'm really digging these quilts. It's putting me in a mood to pull out my sewing machine and whip up a few myself."

Macy shakes her head. "Well, it's inspiring me to whip out my credit card and purchase a few myself. Why aren't any of these for sale, Bizzy? They all say on loan. How about loaning one to your sister? They'd look great in my shop, *and* on my bed."

Georgie pops up before I can answer, and she's wielding Annabeth in that pristine muslin and lace dress of hers. Her head is miraculously adhered right back where it belongs, and I take a moment to marvel at the fact her hair and face don't look singed in the least.

"Hey? How did you do that?" I ask as Fish takes a swipe at the haunted porcelain among us.

George pulls Annabeth out of Fish's swiping range while rocking the doll like a baby.

"I used some of the epoxy I have for my mosaics and was able to get her head right back onto her body. And look—

not a speck of soot on her. It's as if she never rolled into a firepit last night."

Mom gasps. "My dream!"

"Excuse me for a second," I say as I shuttle Macy off to the side. "Any luck with the man in the trench coat last night?"

Her expression sours. "Nope. He and that chick he was with looked as if they were arguing, and as soon as he pitched those flowers onto ground bloody zero, he stalked off good and ticked. If I've learned anything about men, it's that there are only so many cliffs you can walk them back from, and anger isn't one of them. But don't worry. I found a handsome monster to occupy my time with. Where are you headed next with your investigation? If it's a hot spot for men who like to play dress-up with fangs or fur, count me in."

"What happened to the monster?"

"He turned into an accountant at midnight."

Annabeth peers from over my shoulder and just about gives me a heart attack.

"Count me in, too," Georgie chimes while rattling the doll.

My phone bleats, and I pull it out. "It's a text from Camila. It looks like we're headed to a club called the Snake Pit tonight to speak to the very next suspect on our list."

A dark laugh strums from my sister. "It looks as if a slithering good time will be had by all. I'll be there with hell's bells on."

Georgie nods. "And I'll be there with this little hell's angel." She gives Annabeth another rattle.

"Lovely," I say.

And I'll be there with my proverbial magnifying glass in hand.

I have a feeling I'm about to get everywhere with Sabrina Ames.

And hopefully, she'll land me right in front of the killer.

Sprinkles pokes her head out of the tote bag I've landed her in and gives a quick look around at the club we've just ventured into.

Tell me again why I had to be here?

I pull the cute pooch close. "Because she might jar a memory in you. Or you might evoke feelings of warmth in Sabrina toward Blair, and she might just be willing to spill some valuable information she was otherwise holding back."

Jasper is still at work, but I'm far from alone. Both Georgie and Juni dressed for the clubbing occasion. Georgie has on the requisite black kaftan with a giant beaded pumpkin that sits over her back like an orange bullseye.

Juni is dressed like a cat on the prowl with nothing more than a few strips of leather and well-placed lace. And true to her word, my sister dressed like a vixen who knows how to wield a mean whip. I suppose there's no better means to express her personality. At least this way, the men she meets will know what they're getting into.

Camila is here, of course, sans a costume, with the exception of wearing a kitten ears headband. And in an odd twist of fate, I happened to have donned an identical headband myself. I'm not sure what it says about us, the way we've been twinning as of late, but it's safe to say Camila has great taste in both men and fashion.

The Snake Pit is tucked in the armpit of Edison, the cooky spooky town not far from Cider Cove, and indeed this cloistered club is slithering with bodies. It's dimly lit, save for the swirling red and purple lights overhead. The music is thumping, and the scent of funny cigarettes and grilled burgers fills the air.

There are so many bodies moving and grooving to the obnoxiously loud beat that we inadvertently find our way on the dance floor as the entire room explodes with gyrating limbs.

A man with a colorful Mohawk accidentally plows into Juni, and she yelps out the word *ouch* so loud it creates an echoing effect as other revelers decide to mimic her.

"Watch where you're going," she snips to the tall man with high cheekbones and a wall of muscles for a body. "That hurt." She clasps her hand over her shoulder.

"Sorry." He seems sincere in his apology. "But a little pain is good for you." He gives a quick wink while bopping back into the crowd.

Georgie shakes her head while looking to that haunted doll she insisted on hauling down with us. "Spoken like a man who probably owns a riding crop," she muses, and both Macy and Juni exchange a wild-eyed look.

"Here's hoping," Macy says before she ducks into the crowd after him.

"Hey!" Juni calls out. "I touched him, he's mine," she shouts while in hot pursuit of my sister.

"Well, I'm going to lick him!" Macy calls back.

Camila snorts while nodding to Georgie. "You made quick work of that." She glances to Annabeth. "I take it you brought the terrifying toy along to keep the freaks and geeks at bay."

Georgie makes a face. "Freaks and geeks just so happen to be my people. In fact, I'm hoping to bring a few home with me. Now where's the killer, Bizzy? If you can't get her to shake out the murderous details, I'll sic Annabeth after her."

Camila chortles. "And Bizzy, you can sic that little purse puppy you brought along. I'm sure Sabrina will be shaking in her pleather boots. It's a miracle you've solved any cases at all."

Sprinkles whimpers. *I don't think you should sic me on anyone. I'm a lover, not a fighter. See any available four-legged men in here? I like them fuzzy around the face.* She does her best to crane her neck while inspecting the place. *Blair always did say that nothing set a romantic mood better than music.*

"Sorry, Sprinkles." I give her furry little head a quick pat. "You just might be the only dog in the building."

"Not true." Camila snorts. "I've been to this club before and dealt with a few of these men. Believe me when I say, there are plenty of dogs in this place tonight." She gives a wild wave. "Sabrina!" No sooner does she call out her friend's name than Sabrina Ames is wrapping her arms around the precocious pussycat in front of me.

Sabrina is decked out to the reptilian nines, sporting very little else other than her body paint. She has on a two-piece swimsuit of some kind, but it's her colorful arms and legs that steal the show with the intricately drawn rose trellis filled with red poms climbing up her body. The roses are so detailed they look as if you could pluck one right off her body. Not to mention the thorns look as if they're in motion to do something sinister. She really is a walking work of art.

"So glad to see you both." She gives me a friendly wave before she spots Annabeth, and her mouth falls open. "Wow, that's creepy. And she looks old, too."

"Mind your manners, young lady." Georgie pulls Annabeth close. The look on her face lets us know she's affronted. "Annabeth says she thinks *you* look creepy and old."

Perfect. Just what I need. Georgie and her haunted doll having a confrontation with my suspect before I ever get the chance to say six words.

I pull a tight smile as I look to Sabrina. "It's a creature of comfort to her. She doesn't go anywhere without that haunted little thing. Speaking of little things, I've brought Sprinkles along." I swing the tote bag toward my chest as Sprinkles' little head pokes out. "We're having a great time together."

"Aw," Sabrina coos. "I just know Blair would have loved that you're taking such good care of her little girl." *Ironic since Blair had no idea how to take care of anyone except herself. I bet the little dog is relieved she's gone. Billy is glad—that's for darn sure.*

My lips invert in an effort to keep from calling her out on her little meetup with Billy yesterday.

Camila heads toward her rose-strewn friend. "Speaking of Blair, who was this Dr. Feel Good she kept telling me about? I'm in the mood for a little comfort myself, but I don't care too much for dolls or dogs, if you know what I mean. I'm looking for a body to keep me warm at night. And if I'm right, he's ripe for the pickin'."

She and Sabrina share a lively cackle.

"Boy"—Sabrina sweeps her eyes up and down Camila—"you haven't changed one bit. Still on the hunt for something tall, dark, and delicious you could really sink your teeth into." *As if I'm going to send Camila in Billy's wily direction. Nope, that's one dog who needs to pay for what he's done, and I'd hate to see Camila get caught up in that mess.*

Pay for what he's done? It sounds as if Sabrina is convinced he's the killer. And to be honest, I'm right there with her.

Georgie leans toward Sabrina. "You'd better give this girl what she wants." She hitches her thumb to Camila. "I've seen her go hungry when it comes to men, and it's not pretty. If her appetite for male destruction isn't satiated soon, she might just go after your man. She's been after Bizzy's man for a while and *she's* married to the guy."

Sabrina belts out a laugh that transcends the raucous music. "Still up to your old tricks, huh, Camila?" She looks to Georgie. "Don't mind her. She's already stolen six of my boyfriends and we've survived the fallout. But I'm single now, so I can tolerate her a bit better." She gives a playful wink. "And I guess you're right." She shrugs to Camila.

"Blair's old boyfriend is single now, too. But he's still licking his wounds. I can introduce you to the head bartender if you like. He's not only dressed like a werewolf, but he's been known to howl at the moon both in and out of costume. Trust me when I say, he's a hot commodity."

Georgie grunts, "Hold the kid, Bizzy." She shoves Annabeth into my arms and Sprinkles yelps at the sight of her. "I'm suddenly thirsty for a man who knows how to howl." She zips for the bar like a bolt of silver-haired lightning.

"That was subtle," I say as I look to Sabrina. "Speaking of subtle"—I do my best to cringe—"I'm dying to know why Blair called her boyfriend Dr. Feel Good. I mean, I get the obvious implication, but I was wondering if there was a deeper meaning behind it. Like maybe he's a physician?"

Sprinkles chirps, *She never called him by his name, Bizzy. She once said his true name couldn't be spoken in order to protect the identities of all parties involved.*

All parties involved?

"He's no doctor." Sabrina scoffs as if it were far-fetched. "He's a professor at Rose Glen Community College."

"Oh? My sister went there," I tell her. "What does he teach?"

"Psych classes." She shrugs. "You know what they say, it takes a nut to know one. Although, I think we could all agree Blair was equally as insane." She blinks my way. "If you knew Blair the way Camila and I did, you'd see that was almost a compliment."

Sprinkles whimpers. *Sounded like nothing but an insult to me.*

Me too. But I guess I didn't know Blair.

Camila nods. "But her legacy lives on. I spoke to Tabitha this morning, and she said her dinner party is set for six this Friday night." She lifts her brows as she looks my way. "I suggested the Country Cottage Café."

"Perfect," I say. "I can have a private area set up out on the patio. I'll have heat lamps so we won't freeze to death."

"Ooh." Sabrina wiggles her shoulders. "That sounds like it's going to be fun. You ladies are going to love it. I can't wait until all the details are revealed."

"Speaking of Friday," I say. "I have a booth open for your makeup tutorial this Friday afternoon if you're up for it. We've got every school in the area coming out to do a field trip, and there will be plenty of parents there, too. Just tell me what I owe you."

"Friday is perfect. And I don't charge for tutorials. I hand out business cards and make my real money doing parties. But if you can bring a few of those jack-o'-lantern hand pies my way, that would be payment enough. I had one that first night, and I've been craving them ever since." She reaches over and gives Annabeth's cheek a quick pinch. "I'd like to take a bite out of this creepy little cutie, too. She'd be a great prop at the booth."

The lights go out for a moment, and the music cuts out, leaving us in pitch darkness with nothing but the sound of *oohs* and *ahhs* circling the room before the lights and music spring back to life.

"Shoot." Sabrina cranes her neck past me. "I'd better check out the electrical panel—and make sure the generator is ready to go in the event that happens again. I'll catch up with you two later."

Camila shudders. "You don't think that haunted doll had anything to do with that electrical outage, do you?"

"You bet your spooky kooky socks she did."

Sprinkles barks. *Quick, get me home before she hacks off my head and lands it in the nearest fire.*

We gather up Georgie, Macy, and Juni—and our party grows by one colorful Mohawk. I say goodnight to Camila as the rest of us head back to the frightmare taking place at the Country Cottage Inn.

No thanks to Sabrina, I've got a little homework to do tonight, and it very much involves some digging into the faculty at the Rose Glen Community College.

Oh, Billy boy, Billy boy, what have you done?

Hold onto your trench coat because I'm about to find out.

13

Rose Glen Community College is tucked away among a virtual forest of maple trees.

It seems whoever designed the landscape of this institute of higher learning really loved punchy-colored fall leaves. Either that, or they had an affinity for skeletal branches. Macy and I wade our way through a thicket of leaves as we hike across campus all the way into the warmth of the administration building.

I decided that bringing Camila along for this little outing wasn't necessary, and for sure I wasn't about to extend the invite to Georgie and her haunted new BFF. Nope, this would be weird enough all on its own. And there was no way I was going to bring Sprinkles.

If this man did kill Blair, the sight of her dog might make him clam up—or make him think that Blair is haunting him from the other side. And if he did the murderous deed, she should be.

The inside of the administration building is festooned with ghosts and spiders in keeping theme with the upcoming holiday. It's light and bright and a few students sit on sofas off to the right, looking somewhat studious while staring at their phones.

Macy looks around. "All of the hotties have their offices on the second floor," she whispers. "I did a little digging myself, and it turns out, there's an admittance counselor who looks as if he could be Johnny Depp's doppelgänger. I'm going to head on up and see if the wench in me can bring out the pirate in him. Don't do anything goofy like get yourself decapitated."

"Right back at you," I say as I follow her up the steel and concrete staircase leading to the second level. "Professor Helsing is upstairs, too, and I'm just in time for his office hours."

There are only two psych professors at this campus. One is a woman and the other a man who looks to be in his mid-thirties named Dr. William Helsing—aka Billy.

Jasper helped in the endeavor, and we couldn't believe how easy he was able to dig up the information we needed. I didn't tell him that I'd be attempting to speak with Billy boy this afternoon. Instead, I lunged right into a few distracting kisses that led to far more interesting distractions.

Let's hope my questioning of this suspect goes off just as easily as tracking him down did.

Macy swats me on the arm. "There's my mark." She nods to the office straight ahead. "Wish me luck." She rides her eyes up and down my body a moment. "You're not exactly a student. Maybe you should have brought that haunted doll of Georgie's as an icebreaker."

"Believe me, it would short-circuit the conversation. In the event you haven't noticed, that little pint-sized menace seems to have the capability to make the lights go on and off at will."

"Really? Who knew I'd have so much in common with a doll?" A crooked smile sharpens over her features. "If all goes well, you'll have to hitch a ride home on your own broom." She charges into the office before I can protest.

Shoot. I knew I should have driven.

A directory sits next to the elevator, and I quickly find Professor Helsing's name and discover he's in office 206. My feet saunter in the direction of his office, and I follow the numbers along the office doors until I hit the jackpot.

A young man with a backpack barrels out of the room, and without putting too much thought into it, I give a light knock on the opened door.

"Excuse me?" I lean my head in, only to find the exact same man I bumped into the day of the murder looking up at me from behind his desk with beady light eyes and a dark beard clipped close to this face. He seems handsome enough, serious enough, too, but despite that, his lips curve my way with an amicable smile.

"Can I help you?"

This is the part where I ask for directions, then segue into how familiar he looks. And I'm about to do just that when I spot an all too familiar haunted doll seated on the chair in the corner, same muslin gown, same haunted face.

"*AAGHH!*" The scream rips from me, harsh and unexpected, and I end up scaring myself all the more.

"Whoa." He gives a light laugh as he quickly makes his way around his desk. "It's just a doll, I promise."

"What's she doing here?" I shriek. Although at this point, the question is more or less rhetorical. It's obvious what she's doing here—what she's been doing all along—stealing my sanity.

"It's just a silly Halloween decoration." He waves her off in an attempt to calm me down. "I share an office with a woman who teaches the art classes, and she enjoys putting out a few holiday touches now and again. She says the doll belonged to her grandmother. She hauls her out every year. I promise she's harmless."

My heart wallops over my chest as if to contest the idea.

I take a moment to squint over at the porcelain beast, and come to think of it, Annabeth has red hair, and this smiling little terror has blonde tresses. Well played, Annabeth. Well played.

He leans in, trying to break my gaze. "What was it that you were about to ask?"

"Oh"—I'm momentarily thrown and can't for the life of me remember my cover—"my sister, um, she's here somewhere." Good grief. This is a disaster. Maybe I *should* have brought Annabeth. At least that way I wouldn't look like such a loon. "The doll seated in the corner looks like a replica of one at the inn I manage. We're actually hosting a haunted roadshow in the event your colleague would be interested."

"What inn?" He lifts a brow. *I've certainly spent my fair share of time at them as of late.*

"The one in Cider Cove, the Country Cottage Inn."

"Oh, the one with all the Halloween activities." Any trace of a smile quickly dissipates. *Small world.*

"Yes, that's the one. We're hosting the town's Halloween Festival, which might explain the reason I'm so jumpy. It's certainly not business as usual in my neck of the woods. In fact, it's been downright scary."

"So I've heard. I'm familiar with the venue." He takes a deep breath as his gaze falls to the floor. "A friend of mine was killed there."

"You knew the girl?"

Wow, everything about William Helsing is seemingly falling into place.

Hey? Maybe he'll confess, and this entire case will wrap up this afternoon. Stranger things have happened—like me stumbling upon Annabeth's long-lost haunted sister.

"I did," he's quick to add. "She was a student of mine."

"I'm so sorry to hear it. I still can't believe she met with such a violent end. You mentioned you were friends, did she ever say anything about having trouble with anyone? I mean, a horrific event like that couldn't have just come up out of the blue."

"It could with Blair." He slaps the back of his neck as he bounces his brows. "She had a bit of a polarizing personality."

"Oh? Hard to get along with?"

"No, not that." He dismisses the idea with a shake of the head. "She was actually very easy to get along with." *Because she was manipulative as the day was long.* "Let's just say she liked to get her way." *I let her get just that for far too long. And look where it cost me? Or nearly cost me, I should say.*

"I see." I nod. "I have a sister who is the exact same way. I guess some people are just born to lure others into their schemes."

"Schemes?" He tips his ear my way. *She's not one of Blair's ridiculous Midnight Maidens, is she?* "Did you know Blair?"

179

"Not at all. Like I said, I just run the inn. I did interact with her briefly when she was picking up her ticket." Here's my chance. "She mentioned something odd, though, something about meeting her Maidens." I snap my fingers and do my best to look confused. "Something about midnight. Midnight Maidens? Did she ever mention anything about that to you?"

His eyes widen a notch as he shakes his head. "Nope."

It's best I steer clear of both my relationship with the deceased and her dicey dinner party dealings. I couldn't believe what she told me about that little societal farce of hers when she gave me the details. It's sad to see she was probably recruiting more members that night. Leave it to Blair to be greedy right to the bitter end.

Darn it. He's not budging. Although he did mention something about her recruiting for this societal farce.

I guess I'll have to wait until tomorrow night to find out the details.

"Oh well." I shrug. "It's just such a tragedy that she had to go so young. I mean, she'll never have a chance to get married or have children." I hold up my wedding ring. "Sorry. I just got married, and that's sort of the lens I'm seeing the world through right now." That might be true, but it doesn't mean that I mind steering him to at least think about the child Blair was carrying.

His chest expands as he gazes past me. *Blair wasn't the marrying type—she far better fit the mold of the other woman. I should know, she told me so herself. But what she didn't tell me was that she stopped taking her birth control pills. Blair was about to become a mother, all right, one that I'd have to take care of for the next eighteen years. That little lying witch was willing to take down my marriage and my bank account all in one fell swoop. I'm not sure what I was thinking giving her the cash, but she took it and she said she'd take care of things on her end.*

Ah-ha! He was paying her off to get rid of her and the baby. What a two-timing snake.

"That's okay." He shakes his head as if forcibly pulling himself out of a trance. "Congratulations on the wedding." He offers a sorrowful smile. "My wife and I haven't always seen eye to eye, but let's just say something shifted recently and it has me appreciating my marriage in a whole new light." *If I weren't married, I probably would have flaunted my relationship with Blair. She was young and beautiful, but she was trouble until the very end. And to think I actually considered leaving Stacey for Blair at one point. Good thing Blair and I are over for good. And I don't regret one bit doing my part to ensure that happened.*

I suck in a quick breath, and our eyes lock a moment too long.

There's a knock on the door, and it's a student, a young girl with an innocent look to her. Here's hoping Dr. Feel Good doesn't strike again.

"Thank you for your time," I say as I inch my way backward, and a thought comes to me.

"Halloween is the final night of the festival. And it's the last night we'll have Blair's memorial up if you wanted to come by and take a moment to say goodbye."

He tips his head as if considering the idea. "Maybe I will. Thank you for that."

The student barrels in past me, and I step outside, taking a second to catch my breath.

Why do I feel as if I just spent some time with Blair Bates' killer?

I glance back into the office just as the student chucks her backpack to the floor and the commotion causes Annabeth's blonde twin to give a slow wink my way.

A mean shiver rides through me as I head for the stairs, and I slam right into a tall, vexingly handsome homicide detective that I happen to know on an intimate level.

"Detective Baker Wilder." Jasper offers up a wry smile. "And here I thought I'd cut you off at the chase. I knew I shouldn't have stopped for coffee first."

I give a little shrug. "Good thing you didn't stop for lunch. I'm starving."

I shoot my sister a quick text letting her know that I indeed found a ride home.

Jasper and I head out and enjoy a pizza, just the two of us, no haunted dolls, no mind-reading deputies ready to inadvertently take down the life-long friendship I've built with my bestie, and it's bliss.

Once we get back to the inn, there's an envelope with my name on it waiting for me at the reception desk. I open it up to find a handwritten note that reads,

Some people just don't know when to quit.

Final warning.

Do or die.

14

Another note.

I thought it was funny that the killer is tracking my every move so carefully and yet, Jasper is not as amused. He's ordered an entire precinct of men to cover the grounds here at the Country Cottage Inn, and he's given me strict instructions not to leave the property.

Jasper says he's got a few leads that might be able to crack this case wide open, but when I pressed him for what they might be, he just offered a wry smile and told me to pick out a few pumpkins for us. He said he was in the mood to carve a couple out for our first Halloween as a married couple.

Of course, I thought that was adorable. But I was equally vexed. I shared all of the information I've gleaned on the case with him. But then, to be fair, he probably realizes if something he tells me inspires me to leave the grounds of the inn, I'd bolt faster than a greyhound pouncing on a juicy streak. I can't help it, it's my nature to want to get to the bottom of things—especially murder.

The clouds hang bleak overhead as the afternoon festivities get underway at the Fall-oween Festival, and I head right over to the craft booths set up next to the midway. A thick crowd congregates in the vicinity, mostly mothers whose children are running wild through the fairgrounds. I've got Fish in my arms and both Sprinkles and Sherlock at my feet.

Sherlock barks. *Jasper and I agree. We can't wait for this circus to be over. We miss the peace and tranquility of the inn.*

"Tomorrow's Halloween," I tell him. "The last big haunted hurrah."

Sprinkles gives a little yip. *How I hope I haven't overstayed my welcome. Where will I go from here? What's to become of me?*

"Oh, you tiny little cutie." I reach down and give her a quick scratch. "You're not going anywhere until we find you a forever home. I don't care how long that takes. You'll be safe with me."

Look, Bizzy. Fish twitches in my arms. *I see your sister.*

Sure enough, Macy stands in front of Raven Marsh's table, and by the looks of all of those colorful beakers and exotic looking bottles, my sister is having a one-of-a-kind potion concocted in hopes to snag a man. Not that Macy needs the aid of any perfume to tackle the testosterone laden among us.

I quickly head over.

"Hey, Macy," I say as I spot two more familiar faces. "Raven and Sabrina." I give a little wave with Fish's paw. "How's it going, ladies?"

"Busy." Raven looks up, and the dark bun sitting on her head gives a wobble. "I'm almost sold out of my goods."

A wooden sign set out in front of her reads, *The Potion Perfumery, scents guaranteed to seduce. All Sultry Scents, twenty percent off today only!*

Macy smears a smile my way. "She's almost sold out, thanks to me."

Raven bubbles with a laugh. "Thank you, indeed. I think you're going to have all the men in Cider Cove falling at your feet." ***If I had more customers like this, I could retire early. I wish women understood that they held the power to attract a man and there isn't a cosmetics-based variable that makes a difference— certainly not my perfume. But if they need a little liquid courage by way of my perfume, then so be it.***

If they need it to feel seen, then I'll happily take their green.

Sabrina pauses a moment while painting a child's face to lean our way.

"Hey, Bizzy!" Her pale eyes glint my way as she grins. Sabrina has the type of smile that lights up her whole face. But her eyes—they have a smile all their own as if they were in some big secret—like the Midnight Mavens, I'm guessing. I bet she's knee-deep in that secret society. "This is so much fun. I wish I would have come by a little more often this month." *But after tomorrow night, I'm never going to look at Cider Cove again.*

I can't help but laugh at the honesty. She has a line of children, thirteen deep, and every last one of them looks anxious to have their faces turned into a work of art.

"Wow," I marvel at the little girl before her with her face transforming into a purple dragon right before my very eyes. "You are amazing, Sabrina. Where did you learn to do that?"

She chuckles. "I don't know about amazing. But I took a few classes here and there. I had a boyfriend who worked nights, so while he was occupied I thought I'd occupy myself."

"Nice work," Macy muses. "Did the skills you picked up in those classes outlast the boyfriend?"

Sabrina laughs as she cuts my sister a look. "Yup. We had a real love-hate relationship. And I guess it's still going. As much as I hate him, he's the reason I'm doing what I love."

Fish groans. *I bet she doused herself in those perfumes for him, too. Doesn't Macy see she's handing over her money to a charlatan?*

Macy picks up an emerald bottle. "Catnip?" she says, reading the label as Fish scrambles out of my arms.

Let me smell it, let me smell it! She gives a hair-raising yowl.

"I have a feeling that one is coming home with me," I say as Macy hands it my way, and Fish all but falls into an instant catnip coma.

Raven laughs. "Let me whip up a little something for you, too, Bizzy. I have a good feeling about this."

Macy scoffs. "*Please*. She's married. She doesn't even need to shower anymore."

Raven cuts a quick look my way. *Yes, she is married. Camila told us all about it. That homicide detective is one hot side of beef. Some girls get all the luck.* She openly scowls my way before getting back to the task at hand.

Raven gives me a short quiz on my favorite scents, and the scents that Jasper might like, and soon enough, I've handed over some serious cash—far more than I care to think about—in exchange for two bottles. One for Fish and one for me to seduce my husband. Not that Jasper cares if I'm wearing perfume. Come to think of it, he prefers I not wear anything.

Sabrina flashes a smile my way. "It looks as if you'll have one happy husband."

Macy groans. "Believe me, he's happy. They're both delirious. They just got back from their honeymoon." She pretends to retch.

"Nice." Sabrina turns around. *Honeymoon? Maybe that's why the detective hasn't made his arrest yet. His head isn't in the game. I mean, the clues are right in front of him. Blair was knocked up. You have to figure he has this information by now. If I were Billy, I'd be quaking in my two-timing boots.*

I nod over to her as if she said those words out loud. Sabrina thinks Billy did this. And I'd have to agree with her.

Sherlock barks up at me. *I don't want a perfume that smells like bacon. I just want bacon, Bizzy.*

I reach into my pocket and toss both him and Sprinkles a tiny treat. It may not be bacon, but neither of them seems to be complaining.

Sprinkles gives a happy little bark. *Raven used to give me treats all the time when Blair visited her at the salon. And Sabrina used to feed me right off her plate whenever I spent the weekend with her. She*

would watch me while Blair and Dr. Feel Good had their getaways.

"Well, that was very nice of her," I whisper.

Macy nods. "I know, right? She gave me two bottles for free." She shrugs as she collects her haul. "I'll let you ladies know how I fare. I plan on bathing in this tomorrow night. And I'll be right back here putting it to the test. Let's hope I get a vampire who knows how to bite in all the right places."

We share a laugh as a crowd moves in.

I give both Raven and Sabrina a wave. "I'll see you girls tonight!" I can't wait for this shroud of secrecy to end.

And that's exactly what I'm hoping will happen.

It's Friday evening, heavy auburn and purple clouds hang above us in the angry sky, and the twinkle lights have lit up every inch of the acreage around the Country Cottage Inn, casting an enchanted glow over the land. The pumpkin patch set to the left of the cove is the busiest I've yet seen it— as it should be, considering tomorrow is the spookiest day of the year. And there are not one but two bounce houses set up next to those happy orange globes.

The west side of the property is brimming with bodies as well, each one of them in costume as the evening revelry gets underway. And every now and again couples make their way down to the waterline with a stuffed bear that was just won from the midway.

Emmie and Jordy helped me set up an elongated table along the back patio of the Country Cottage Café, and Jordy even spent the day adding a few more twinkle lights so we would have enough light for our dinner party.

Emmie said she would work the table for me just to make sure we receive the best service. I may have let my bestie in on the fact that a few suspects were afoot. And I may have heard her promise Jasper that she'd keep a careful eye on me as he left the café this morning.

It's just a few minutes until six and Fish, Sherlock, and Sprinkles and I have just arrived at the cove. I've bundled up in jeans, my coziest fluffy sweater, and threw a heavy black peacoat on over that. I dug up an orange and black scarf my grandmother knitted for me when I was still in college, and it adds just the right festive appeal to an otherwise drab outfit. I bet Camila will show up looking like a supermodel in some ridiculous off-the-shoulder couture dress.

No sooner do I have the thought than Camila comes up the walk wearing jeans and a black peacoat with an orange and black striped scarf.

A hard groan emits from her once she spots the fashion debacle.

"We have got to stop with the Bobbsey Twins act." She glowers my way as she says it, and Fish hisses up at her from the ground.

"You're so right." I take her in and marvel at how identical our accouterments are right down to the tall black boots. "You've heard of people sending memos to dress alike? We're going to have to send memos to stop this nonsense."

Look at her, Fish grouses. *She's trying to be you, Bizzy. I bet she's been sending all those threatening notes, too.*

Sprinkles barks and her little head bobs wildly as she looks up at Camila. *I'd bite her ankles, but she's got leather boots on. I've chewed through a few of Blair's boots, but it took some time. How much time do we have, Bizzy?*

I shake my head down at the cute pooch in hopes to avoid the shoe-pocalypse.

Sherlock joins in on the barking. *I'll chase her to the water and push her in for you. I've been wanting to do that for a very long time, Bizzy. She was never nice to me when she was with Jasper. And I've never forgotten. I'll show her who's a dumb dog. Let me at her.*

"Down, boy," I say as I give him a quick pat. "It's almost showtime," I say to Camila. "Feel free to ask questions, and no matter what this ludicrous secret society of theirs entails, we're going to agree with whatever the terms are. We need to stay close until we can figure out who the killer is." I texted her and let her know everything I found out about the naughty professor. Camila said she wasn't surprised. Apparently, Blair had a thing for men that were taken. And because of that, it became all too clear what they had in common.

"Sounds good." She glances past me. "You're not having those two loons join us tonight, are you?"

"Georgie and Juni?" I shake my head. "No way. I need this to run smoothly with as little distraction as possible."

Her expression sours as she glares at something over my shoulder.

"Let the games begin!" a familiar squawk emits from behind, and my eyes widen as I see not just Georgie, but that pint-sized poltergeist, and Juni heading this way—and right on their heels are Sabrina Ames, Tabitha Carter, and Raven Marsh.

Sabrina has on a sleek leather jacket and matching pants, her eyes glow in this light—they're almost as silver as Jasper's—and I wonder if that's what our daughter's would look like if we had one.

Tabitha has her hair pulled back and looks a little more dressed up than I've seen her before, with a long dark coat and frilly yellow blouse on underneath. Her face is made up with heavy swaths of cosmetics, lots of mascara giving her that spider lash look and red lipstick, thick as icing.

Raven is bundled in a black Sherpa fur coat, and her long rhinestone earrings glitter in this dull light like stars.

Georgie does an odd little dance as she heads this way, rattling Annabeth in our direction as if she were a maraca.

"Cha-cha, cha-cha cha, *cha!*" She gives a little hop, and her bright orange kaftan gleams under the twinkle lights like a well-lit pumpkin. "I see you eyeing it." She gives her dress a quick pluck. "It's wool. And believe me when I say, it was tough to find this sort of craftsmanship, but don't you worry. I can read your mind, Bizzy Baker. I'll make sure there's one waiting for you under the tree this Christmas."

Camila chortles. "Now that sounds like a threat."

Juni grunts, "Tell me about it. I've received one every year ever since I was three."

Georgie waves her off. "And you were a better kid because of it. Now, where do we sit?"

"Sit?" I look wide-eyed as Tabitha laughs at the thought.

"Sit anywhere you want," she practically sings out the words, and I'm starting to wonder if Georgie and Juni crashed our party on *purpose*—as in, they were invited.

Sabrina, Tabitha, and Raven all give a friendly hello, and I snag a chair from a neighboring table and soon the seven of us are seated.

Emmie comes over and quickly furnishes each of us with a beverage, and we order several trays of appetizers before putting in our requests for our meals. Typically, the café isn't a full-service sit-down restaurant, but since this is a special event, we're going the extra service mile.

Raven looks my way. "Bizzy, any word on who could have done this to Blair? I feel like so much time has passed. I'm shocked they haven't made an arrest by now." *Not that I think they'll be arresting anyone anytime soon.*

My mouth opens as I try to digest her odd thought.

"No," I say. "Not that I know of."

Tabitha tips her head my way. "Are they close? I mean, Raven is right. Time is passing us by. If they don't solve this soon, this is going to be a cold case." *That's what I'm hoping for. Just because Blair is gone, doesn't mean the Maidens need to suffer. God forbid someone starts digging in this direction. It could ruin everything. I need the Maidens. I sure as heck didn't need Blair.*

She didn't need Blair? Is that a confession?

Sabrina shrugs. "I'm confident they'll find whoever did this. I mean, Camila, you brought up Bizzy's lucky streak when it comes to tracking down killers."

"Lucky nothing," Georgie grouses. "She's an evil genius when it comes to evil geniuses. If anyone can winnow out the killer, Bizzy can."

Tabitha raises a brow. "Well then, we'd better speed things along so we can get you back out there. After we have *our* dessert, maybe you can give the killer their *just desserts.*"

A soft round of laughter circles the table.

Tabitha shares a knowing glance to Sabrina. ***It's time. I really hope I don't botch this up. And boy, am I ever glad Blair isn't here to witness it. At least I've got two women. And Raven had to get two as well. But that's not such a bad thing. Blair always did say we need a few spares. Just because you have a warm body in front of you, doesn't mean they're going to say yes.***

Sabrina averts her eyes. ***Oh, come on already. It's painful watching Tabitha crash and burn like this. If Blair had one rule, it was never let there be any dead airtime. And it really ticks me off. If she doesn't pull it together fast, I'll be losing money, too.***

Raven clears her throat. "Welcome, everybody." She raises her glass a moment. "To good times and new friends." ***Good gracious, someone had to do it.***

We all raise our glasses as well, and both Georgie and Juni howl as if they've morphed into a couple of werewolves.

Emmie comes out with another tray of appetizers and Georgie motions to her.

"Can I get a highchair for the kid?" Georgie hikes Annabeth up a notch. "She steals from my plate if I let her lap sit."

Fish looks up at me. *I believe her.*

I believe her, too.

"Sure thing." Emmie takes off, as nervous laughter takes over the table. Soon enough, Annabeth's porcelain frame is seated upright in a tiny wooden seat of her own.

I can tell Sabrina is holding back a full-blown laugh as she looks to Georgie. *Now there's a live one. I bet we can milk twice the fee from her.*

Fee?

I shoot Camila a look.

What exactly is going on here? Not that I expect Camila to answer.

She offers a tight smile my way. "So what's the big surprise?" Camila nods to Tabitha. "I'm on pins and needles to hear all of the details." *Let's get on with it already.*

"I'm glad you asked." Tabitha shudders. *Considering I've only done this once before, and that night ended in disaster, I don't have very high hopes that this night will end any different.* "Before our dear friend Blair Bates passed away, she invited several of her closest friends into a private society called the Midnight Maidens."

"*Ooh.*" Juni gasps. "A secret society! Who gets to sleep in the casket first?" She raises her hand to the sky. "If there's grave digging involved, I call dibs on the jewelry of the deceased." She leans toward her mother. "You know they only put on the best for those dirt naps."

"Juni." Georgie rolls her eyes. "Everyone knows you bury 'em with fakes." She leans toward Tabitha. "But if there's a jewelry heist involved somehow, I call dibs on holding the weapon."

Tabitha and Raven share a warm laugh, but Sabrina isn't all that entertained by the idea.

"There's no jewelry heist." Sabrina gives a long blink. "That I can promise." She looks to Camila and me. "But there is a celebration that involves cash prizes, and I think you girls will be especially interested."

Tabitha nods. "The Midnight Maidens are sort of like a unique birthday party. Wouldn't you ladies like to have a party thrown in your honor more often?"

Georgie grunts, "Not if it means I age twice as fast, sister. I've only got so many numbers to go before my number is up, and that's one finish line I'm not racing toward."

Raven laughs. "Heavens no. It's like a birthday without any aging involved. In fact, if anything, you'll feel rejuvenated once it's your turn."

Tabitha nods. "It's a gifting circle. An investment, really. And the reason I called the four of you here tonight to tell you about it is because you all look so smart." *Wait. Was I supposed to say smart? Or did the script say business savvy? Oh heck, never mind.*

"A gifting circle?" Camila taps her red polished fingernails along her glass as she brings it toward her. "So how does this work?"

Tabitha's lips waver with a nervous smile. "First, I'll tell you how it all started. Blair's real estate business was doing pretty well, but she knew there had to be a way to earn a little extra cash. One night she came up with an entrepreneurial program that was guaranteed to work, and more importantly, guaranteed to empower women. And being the kind, generous person she was, she wanted to include her friends in on it—thus the Midnight Maidens were born. Each Maiden eventually brings in just two more Maidens, and within a few weeks, we each have a gifting circle party thrown in our honor."

Georgie leans in. "Count me in, Toots. I love a good party. I'd like chocolate cake at mine. And maybe some of those cops who show up pretending to arrest you right before they take all your clothes off."

"You mean their clothes off," I tell her.

"I mean my clothes. No offense, but it sounds like you go to the wrong parties, Biz."

She got one part right. The cops are bound to show up.

Juni raises her hand. "And I'd like to go next. I've got a hot weekend coming up with a man with a Mohawk. Let's just say I expect things to get pretty wild. I'll need all the empowerment I can get just to keep up with him."

Raven chortles. "You ladies are a hoot. But you can't go next."

Sabrina makes wild eyes her way. "Not to worry." She offers a forced grin to both Georgie and Juni. "You'll be coming up very, very soon." She glowers over at Tabitha. "Why don't you tell them about the hierarchy of the nobility?"

"Oh, right." Tabitha clears her throat. "Okay, first you start off as a countess, then at the next gifting circle party you'll bump up to a duchess. Wait...is that right?" She glances to Sabrina and Sabrina looks fit to kill.

"Ooh, me *me*!" Georgie raises her hand this time. "I had a hot Marine call me his duchess for about six weeks in the summer of '69. I think that bumps me up a notch automatically."

Sabrina gives a nervous laugh. "Not quite yet. But you'll get there soon enough."

Tabitha nods. "And after that, you'll be a princess, then a queen."

I think I'm seeing a much clearer picture here.

I nod to Tabitha. "And what happens once you're a queen?"

She presses her lips tightly a moment as if she had a secret she was bursting at the seams to tell us.

"Of course, there is only *one* queen." Tabitha draws in a breath. "And when it's your turn, you'll be celebrated in a very special way."

Juni holds up the mini bagel pizza bite in her hand. "And that's when you'll get to sleep in the casket. I've seen this movie!"

"No casket." Raven laughs. "But lots and lots of money." She nods to Tabitha. ***It's time.***

"Right." Tabitha looks as if she's holding her breath at this point. "We all need to participate a little financially, but don't think of it as giving money away. You'll be gifting it to a friend. And then, when it's the day of your coronation ceremony, we'll all gather and shower you with gifts."

Camila gives Raven a shifty-eyed glance. "Monetary gifts?"

"That's right." Raven nods. "Believe me, Camila, I wouldn't be a part of something cheesy. I can see your antennae going up. This is no scam."

Both Sprinkles and Sherlock Bones run up, barking in unison. ***It's a scam, Bizzy! It's a scam!***

I nod their way because I know it is.

"It's not a scam." Sabrina shakes her head emphatically. "This is women helping women."

"Friends helping friends," Raven is quick to add.

Tabitha reaches her hand across the table toward Camila. "And it works. Blair went through twice and pocketed as much as one hundred thousand dollars." *And I'm so close to having my gifting day. I can't mess this up. If I don't come up with cash soon, I'll lose the roof over my head and have to move into my brother's basement with his horrible wife. God knows I'd do just about anything to keep that from happening.*

"Wait a minute." Georgie squints at the three women before us. "Is this going to land me in the pokey?"

Juni shudders. "I'm in no hurry to get back to that place. Count me out."

It's true. Juni did some time up in Collinsworth Correctional Facility due to unpaid traffic tickets, or something equally as petty yet legally vexing.

Tabitha shakes her head. "It's one hundred percent legal." *Okay, so that's not entirely true, but there's an ironclad loophole that ensures none of us will ever go to prison. If anyone so much as gets close to legal trouble, Blair laid out the perfect cover. We simply tell them we were buying gift cards off of one another. And if I wanted to spend five K on a gift card, who's to stop me? It's not against the law to tip a friend for picking something up for you.*

I nearly choke on the breadstick in my mouth.

My hands grab for my water as I quickly wash it down. "How much of a gift are we expected to bring to the party?" I ask innocently enough as if I didn't just hear the asinine amount. Now let's see if they're bold enough to fess up.

Tabitha holds up a finger. "I'll tell you in a moment. But just remember, you get a forty thousand dollar payday in just a few weeks, so you're not really giving your money away—your friends are merely holding it for you."

Raven nods. "And when they give it back, you'll get far more in return than any bank could ever give you. It's as if we've bested Wall Street."

Sabrina leans in. "And it's just in time for Christmas. Think of the relief it will be when you don't have to worry about a mountain of credit card debt come January."

"Well, I want in." I shrug as if it were true.

"You do?" Georgie eyes me with suspicion.

Fish yowls from somewhere behind the table. *Oh, how I hope you're pulling the wool over these women's eyes. I'd hate to think they were pulling the wool over yours. You do realize I depend on you to keep me in Fancy Beast cat food.*

"I definitely do." I double down on this dumb mess. "Just tell me how much to bring. I don't know about you, Camila, but I can use a big payday right before the holidays."

Tabitha sheds an ear-to-ear grin. "I knew you were a smart group of ladies. And that's exactly why we've called you here."

"Thank you for that," I tell her. "So when's the next party? And how much do we bring?"

Tabitha sharpens her eyes over mine. "Tomorrow, Halloween night, eleven o'clock, right here at the far end of the field near where Blair was slain. There's a small forest that butts right up to it. We'll have an initiation ceremony, and then we'll make the exchange. Be sure to wear a costume. It is Halloween, after all."

"How much?" Camila's tone is a touch too curt because it's not lost on either of us that they're skirting the monetary-based issue.

"Five thousand." Tabitha looks from Camila to me as if trying to read us. "Cold, hard cash only. No checks, no money orders."

Georgie inhales so sharp I'm half-afraid I'll find Annabeth dangling from one of her nostrils. But she's not. However, Georgie is losing color quickly, and I think Juni might already be unconscious.

"We're all in," I say, giving both Georgie and Juni a mildly threatening look that suggests they should play along.

"We'll meet you in the woods at eleven o'clock and we'll have the money."

Good grief. Fish sighs.

"Good gracious," Georgie grunts.

"Good times." Juni lifts her glass as if she's about to make a toast.

"It will be," Tabitha says, mimicking the gesture, and soon we're all raising our glasses. "To friends helping friends."

"Friends helping friends," the rest of us echo.

And people who are pretending to be our friends—who are attempting to bleed us dry.

It's clear now what Blair Bates was up to—a pyramid scheme. And now that I think about it, that money floating around her that night—Jasper mentioned it amounted to five thousand dollars.

Now what are the odds of William Helsing giving her the exact same amount she required from her friends in order to play her con-woman games?

And I think about that all through dinner.

Someone killed Blair.

And I can think of five thousand reasons why.

15

As soon as the three official Midnight Maidens take off, I pull Georgie, Juni, and Camila aside.

"Georgie and Juni, I'll cover your costs. I just need you to play along."

Georgie holds Annabeth close as we huddle under the twinkle lights. We just shared a couple of pizzas and made small talk after Tabitha all but shook us down for five thousand dollars apiece. Not that the other two aren't in on it. They're all as guilty in my eyes for propagating this ridiculous scheme.

"Oh, thank God." Georgie gives Annabeth a rocking squeeze. "With that money I saved, my baby girl can afford to go to college."

Juni swats her on the arm. "Forget the money you saved. Think of the money you'll *earn*." She claps her hands together. "I'm ready for my coronation. I'm going to blow all forty grand on a luxury vacation."

"Can I come with ya?" Georgie bats her lashes at her baby girl.

"Nope." Juni is quick to give the idea the kibosh. "You can't bring your mama, or it's not called a vacation. It's called a Mamageddon."

Georgie makes a face. "Come on, Annabeth. Let's go where we're wanted. I think I hear a caramel apple calling my name."

She takes off, and Juni takes off right after her. "You can't have a caramel apple. The last time, I had to take you to the dentist at midnight. You lost three teeth!"

"I didn't want those three teeth anyway," Georgie howls back.

I step in close to Camila. "What about you? I can spot you if you need it."

"I like my teeth right where they are," she sneers. "And I'm bringing my own cash. The last thing I want is for Jasper to think I'm dipping into his savings account. I was always very independent in our relationship, and I'm not going to start depending on him now. By the way, tomorrow night, I'm dressing as a witch."

"So no costume," I say without missing a beat.

"You're not funny."

"I was kidding." Sort of. "I think I've got a toga I'm going to throw on."

"So you're wearing your wedding dress again." She nods. "That's good. So many women only get one use out of it. It's good to see you're taking the initiative to wear it one more time—and at an appropriate venue."

"Would you hush?" I whisper. "And now look who's the one with the sense of humor. It's not my wedding dress." But it does bear a striking resemblance, come to think of it. "Anyway, we'll do whatever it is they want."

"Fine, but I'd better get my money back, or I'll be looking to you for repayment. You're the one dragging us down this rabbit hole."

"What? You're the one who the sheriff's department has pegged as an official suspect, not me. In fact, I think it was you who came to me for my help."

"Well, boy, am I sorry I ever did that. Not only is it costing me my time, not only have I suffered hair damage no thanks to that shellac it was frozen with the other day—and let's not forget about the clear fashion decline I've entered into ever since I've been sharing air space with you—but the toll it's taking on my sanity and social life is mindboggling."

"And to think I actually thought we were on our way to being friends."

"I've seen your friends, Bizzy. I'd have to walk around in pleather while hauling a porcelain misfit they dug up from 1852. My IQ is over one fifty. I hardly qualify."

I suck in a quick breath and lunge at her, only to be stopped by Leo Granger's arm.

"All right, you two. Party's over." He pulls me back a few steps. "What's going on here, anyway?" He shoots his ex the stink eye.

I bet Leo is secretly pleased he's no longer with this piranha. No wonder he's so smitten with Emmie. She's a breath of fresh air compared to this dust storm.

He counters, *I never hid the fact I was thrilled to be done with her. And yes, I'm quite happy with Emmie.*

Camila twitches as she cinches her purse. "There the two of you go again." She gives an incredulous shake of the head. "Go ahead, talk away out loud where everyone can hear you. I really don't care. I'll be here tomorrow night, Bizzy. And if the killer isn't caught, I want my money back—from *you.*" She takes off in a huff just as an icy gust passes through.

"What was that about?" Leo does his best to hook my gaze.

"She's insane. In fact, I think this whole world is insane. Definitely the suspects in Blair Bates' murder investigation are insane. I hope Jasper is home. I can't wait to discuss my latest find with him. I'll give you a hint, it's regarding something called the Midnight Maidens and involves a pyramid scheme that's going to cost me fifteen grand in cash tomorrow night."

"Geez." He inches back. "You're getting in over your head, Bizzy. I think it's time to hand the reins over to Jasper. Whatever you do, don't go emptying out your bank account."

"Oh, I'm not. I'm taking it from the ground safe right here at the inn. I've got three deposits piling up. Trust me, no one will miss the money. I've already decided to have Jasper bust their little scam tomorrow night, so I know for a fact I'll be putting that money right back where I found it." And if things go sideways, I'll be emptying out my personal account. And that is going to hurt. A lot. Not to mention it will be an expensive lesson to learn when it comes to tangling myself up with Camila. I won't need some psycho to leave me threatening notes. I'll leave one for myself.

Leo frowns as he studies me. "I'm sorry to hear it. I'll make sure things don't go sideways. Speaking of going sideways, we've yet to tell Emmie and she's already onto me. She knows there's something I'm dying to share with her."

"Share it already!" Emmie springs out from the darkness with a bubbling laugh. She tosses her dishrag to the table before heading our way. "All right, you two. Let's have it. Leo, you promised you'd tell me tonight." She tips her head his way and offers up a playful yet stern look. Emmie looks so beautiful tonight, with her dark hair swept into a neat ponytail and her aquamarine eyes glowing in the night. "Come on, Bizzy. You know I hate secrets more than anything."

"That's exactly why I'm hesitant," I mutter, mostly to myself, as I spot Sprinkles and Sherlock running wild on the sand.

Fish bounds over and wraps herself around my ankles as if trying to comfort me.

There, there, Bizzy. Emmie is a strong girl. She's bright and capable. Surely, she'll understand the fact you're able to discern her thoughts. And if she asks why you've never brought it up before, simply tell her it slipped your mind. Let Leo do all of the heavy lifting here.

She's right. Leo nods. *Don't worry about a thing. I've got this, Bizzy.*

"Hey?" Emmie runs her hand between Leo and me as if trying to break a trance. "What's going on? The two of you are starting to scare me." *My word, they're not really having an affair, are they? Or maybe they had one just before Bizzy got hitched? Maybe Leo was her last hurrah? If that were true, I'd have to kill her. And if I killed her, I wouldn't be afraid of getting arrested, because Bizzy would be unable to solve her own homicide. Lord knows you can't count on the Seaview Sheriff's Department to do that.*

Both Leo and I chuckle a little at that one.

"What's so funny?" Her voice grows tense.

"All right." Leo pulls her in and wraps his arms around her. "It's time." He nods my way.

"But Jasper isn't here," I protest.

"I'm here!" a deep voice calls out from behind, and before I know it, my husband's loving arms are pulling me in as he lands a kiss to my temple. "Did I miss it?"

"Nope." Leo looks to Emmie as her eyes widen with anticipation. "Elizabeth Lynn Crosby, I love you more than I have ever thought I could love another human being."

"Yes!" Emmie hops up and down as if she just won the lottery, and I can't help but grimace.

"Wait," I say, trying my best to catch her midflight. "Hold on, Em, let him finish."

"He doesn't have to finish." Emmie's cheeks are pink as she clutches at his hands. "I'm in, Leo. I love you, too. I just know this is right." Her chest palpitates a mile a minute as if she were struggling for her next breath. "Now let's see the ring."

"Good glory," I groan. "Emmie"—I step in and take up her hands—"this isn't a marriage proposal. Although, that's probably right around the corner." I shrug to Leo. "Sorry to spoil things. But this is important, too," I say, looking back at this beautiful girl in front of me. "Emmie, you and I have been best friends for as long as I can remember." I swallow hard, mostly in an attempt to keep the words away, but it doesn't seem to be working. "What Leo wants to tell you involves me, too."

Fish mewls, *I can't look. Someone wake me when it's over.*

Emmie shakes her head as her eyes shift from Leo back to me.

"What's going on?" Every last ounce of her jovial affect has dissipated. "Bizzy, say it now, or I'm leaving and never talking to any of you again." Her voice is sharp and commanding, and if I'm not mistaken, it's shaking with anger, too.

I glance to Jasper and he gives a solemn nod.

"Emmie"—I can't seem to catch my breath—"Leo and I share a very special ability. It's nothing we got from each other. But it's the reason we met about a year ago. Do you remember going to that Halloween party when we were thirteen and I had to leave early because Mackenzie Woods dunked me in a whiskey barrel full of water?"

"How can I forget?" She softens. "You haven't swum in the ocean since. What does that have to do with any of this?"

"Everything. You see, something strange happened to me that day, to my brain. I guess this ability was always lurking under the surface, but for some reason, it became pronounced that day." I close my eyes, and for a second, it feels as if I'm right back in that whiskey barrel struggling to breathe, wondering if I'll make it or not—if I'll ever see my best friend again. And yet, right here at this moment, I'm wondering the very same thing for a whole other reason. "Emmie"—I give a few rapid blinks—"I don't know how or why, but ever since that day, I've been able to read people's minds."

A dull laugh streams from her. "You're kidding, right?" She shakes her head at Leo. "Is this one of those plot twist proposals?"

Leo lets out a heavy breath. "No, it's not, Emmie. What I wanted to tell you before we take that next step together— and I want to, very, very soon—is just that." He hitches his head my way. "Bizzy and I are both something called transmundane. And our gift, listening in on other people's thoughts, is further classified as telesensual. We're not trying to listen in, it's just sort of there. It's not something I share with a lot of people. But I want to share it with you. I want so much more with you in this life, Emmie, but I felt that if I didn't let you in on this big secret of mine, it wouldn't be fair. It wouldn't be real."

Emmie takes a slow step back as she looks from Leo to me.

"I think—I think this has gone too far." Emmie is starting to lose the color in her face. "Jasper, make them stop. I don't think it's funny."

"It's true, Emmie." Jasper offers an apologetic shrug. "I'm sorry. Bizzy just told me about eight months ago. It's not easy to wrap your head around, believe me. I've been in your shoes. But I knew I wanted to build a life with Bizzy. And to do that I had to accept her for who she was and what she was capable of."

Emmie scoffs my way. "Bizzy, come on. If you could read my mind, you would have told me ages ago. We don't keep secrets, remember?"

"Just this one," I say just above a whisper. "I'm sorry, Em. I never wanted you to look at me like a monster. I didn't want things to change between us."

Her eyes glisten with tears. *So you're saying you can hear me now?*

I nod her way and watch as her eyes widen with fright. And in less than a second, she takes off into the night.

Leo bullets after her, and my heart plummets right down to middle earth.

"That went just as well as I thought it would." I shake my head as boiling anger takes over inside of me. "I never should have agreed to it. And now I've ruined everything."

"No, I promise." Jasper pulls me in. "She just needs time."

"What if she needs one hundred years? Face it, Jasper. Nothing will ever be the same between Emmie and me again."

Jasper holds me there in the icy wind for what feels like a lifetime.

"How about we get your mind off of things?" He motions to the sand with his head. "Let's catch up to those dogs and hash a few details out as far as the case is concerned."

And we do just that. I tell Jasper all about Blair's Midnight Maidens and their financial underpinnings, and he closes his eyes a good long while.

"A pyramid scheme," he says as Sprinkles and Sherlock bound between our legs. "So maybe William didn't do it? This certainly opens up an entire slew of different motives."

"And don't forget the physical evidence," I say. "What about that ring that was caught on the button of Blair's shirt?"

"It could have belonged to Blair."

"But she was wearing the exact same ring—more or less. Women double up on a lot of things, but identical rings aren't one of them."

His chest expands as he considers this. "It had a different color stone. The one on her finger was a ruby. The lab said the one caught on her button was a zircon."

"Well, maybe it was hers. Although, when I met her, only the ruby caught my eye. I guess I didn't do an analysis of her fingers, though. So there's that."

"Let's go over the suspects." He gives me a gentle squeeze.

"Okay, we've got William Helsing. We know he cheated on his wife and knocked Blair up. He was paying her off, I saw the cash exchange, or at least I thought that's what he gave her. He wanted her to go away, that much we know. And then there's Tabitha Carter. She's having financial trouble. She admitted it to me, albeit in her mind, that she had it out with Blair in private that night. Maybe she was feeling the squeeze financially as far as the Maidens go? I'm guessing you can only give so much before you want to see some of that money back."

"I'm guessing you're right. What about Raven Marsh?"

"The night of the murder, she made a remark to Blair. She said, go take care of Tabitha—and then her next thought was, and then I'll take care of you."

"Cryptic."

I nod. "She also mentally accused Blair of stealing from her. That could be a motive right there. And then there's Sabrina. That night, she said something about not letting Blair get away with this. Although, I'm not sure what that could have been. And she didn't want to send Camila in Billy's direction—Camila was pretending to be *hot for teacher* before we even knew he was a teacher. But Sabrina wouldn't point us his way. She said she wanted to make him pay for what he'd done. I'm not sure exactly what she meant by that."

"So we have a few question marks. It still feels as if all arrows are pointing in William Helsing's direction. I guess I'll need to hunt him down and have a talk with him."

"You won't have to hunt him down. He'll be here tomorrow night. I let him know it was his last chance to leave flowers at the scene of the crime."

"And the Midnight Maidens will be here as well. It looks as if we're about to have one heck of an eventful Halloween."

"That we are." I wrap my arms around him tightly.

And I've got a niggling feeling that it just might turn out to be a little too eventful, a little too frightful, but hopefully, at the end of the day, it will be filled with justice.

There is going to be a day of reckoning for Blair Bates' killer, and I'm hoping that it's coming this Halloween night.

We head back to our cottage just as Jordy runs up.

"Hey, Biz, Jasper." He nods while pulling an envelope from his jacket. "One of the cottage rentals had this mistakenly delivered to them. It clearly has your address on it. I think the mail carrier just wanted to get off the grounds as soon as possible."

"Can't say I blame 'em. Thanks," Jasper says as he takes the letter. "It's addressed to you."

"Open it." I give his arm a squeeze. "Maybe it's from the Maple Meadows Lodge, demanding we return at once."

"We can only hope," he says.

Our honeymoon destination couldn't have been more perfect. They certainly wouldn't have to twist my arm to get us to go back.

Jasper pulls out the letter and unfolds it to reveal a pale blue sheet of paper with the insignia of a rose at the top of the page. And just below that it reads,

You dig, and you dig, and you dig.
And you've dug your own grave.

16

Emmie has avoided me at every turn today.

She won't reply to my texts either. Fish pointed out that Emmie was ghosting me—a term she picked up on from my sister. An appropriate term, considering the fact today is Halloween.

It was a busy morning at the inn, an even busier afternoon, and now that it's evening, it seems as if the entire state of Maine has drained onto our little sliver of the coast. If the grounds around the Country Cottage Inn had a fire code, we would have broken them an hour ago.

Fish is wearing a tiny pointed hat that Georgie plucked off of one of the decorations at the front of the inn. Sherlock is wearing a baby blue sheet with cutouts around the eyes and snout. It's a costume Georgie whipped up when I told her I didn't plan on dressing the animals up this year. She was incensed at the thought, and immediately took matters into her own creative hands. Of course, she didn't leave Sprinkles high and dry. Georgie dug out a pair of tiny pink angel wings from her closet and strapped them to the tiny Yorkie's back. And just like that, Sprinkles is the cutest fairy of them all.

I'm the star of the show! Sprinkles yips.

"That you are," I say as we slowly navigate the throngs of people.

Every now and again, someone stops us to take a picture with Sherlock and Sprinkles. I've got Fish wrapped in my cloak, so they can't really see how adorable she looks. It turns out, the toga costume was a no-go after I discovered it was perfectly see-through. So I went with the Little Red Riding Hood costume that I found in the back of my closet instead, and dug up an old basket, which Fish is currently cozying up in. Not only was I not in the mood to shop for the animals, I didn't feel like shopping for myself either. That note Jordy handed us last night ruined my appetite for both food and shopping.

The meadow is thick with costumed bodies that range from adorable to downright gruesome. The twinkle lights up above sparkle in the night like their own constellation, and I take in the scene one last time. As chaotic as it's been hosting the event, a part of me is going to miss the madness.

A familiar couple steps into my line of vision, and I can't help but make a face.

"Mayor Woods." I nod to the feisty brunette dressed as a superhero of some kind. She's donned a red and blue leotard with a gold star in the middle of her belly, and she's wearing red tights with a red cape to match. "Hey, Hux." I pull my brother in for a quick embrace. He, too, is dressed as a superhero, although in a far more subtle fashion. He still has his suit on from work, I'm assuming, and he's secured a bright blue cape around his neck.

"Little Red Riding Hood, I see," Mackenzie muses. "Let me guess. You've got a knife in that basket of yours and you're ready to mow down another victim? Boy, you really lucked out when you tricked that homicide detective into marrying you."

"I'm not nearly as coordinated as the two of you," I say. "Let *me* guess, Mack. You're fighting crime on the mean streets of Cider Cove? And Hux, you're doing your part to save the men of this world from snarky women by way of dating one yourself?"

Hux laughs, but Mackenzie smacks him on the arm, and he buttons it up real quick.

"Nice to see she's got you trained." I shrug his way. In the distance, I spot Jasper and Leo heading this way with stern expressions, walking at a quickened clip as if they were men on a mission. "I'll see you two around," I say as I bypass them.

"What's going on?" I ask as I intercept my handsome husband and his deputy counterpart.

Jasper's jaw clenches as he looks to the makeshift memorial in the distance.

"I'm this close to making an arrest." His eyes soften over mine. "We have evidence linking William Helsing to those notes you've been getting."

"I knew it." I hiss

You're always right, Bizzy, Fish mewls.

Both Sherlock and Sprinkles bark with approval.

Leo nods to the back of the clearing. "I see him. Let's make our move."

I glance that way, and sure enough, there he is with his trench coat on, his head bowed in front of the fencing that separates him from the murder site. By the looks of it, he has a bouquet of red roses in his hand.

A breath hitches in my throat. "Are you going to arrest him, right here?"

"No." Jasper doesn't miss a beat.

"If you're not making an arrest, what are you doing with him?" I ask, confused.

Jasper's chest widens a notch. "Taking him down for questioning. I think I can strong-arm a confession out of him. That rose insignia on the letter we got last night belonged to Rose Glen Community College. The school confirmed it's a part of their unofficial letterhead. All the pieces to the puzzle are there."

Leo nods. "With the exception of the biggest piece of them all—a confession."

"Don't wait up." Jasper lands a kiss just above my ear. "I'll have a treat for you when I get home."

"I'll keep the cape on and not much else." I give a little wink. "Good luck with everything. As soon as you get a confession, let me know."

They take off like bullets, and I follow a safe distance behind. I sure as heck don't want to be there when they're strong-arming him to the station, but it doesn't mean I want to miss the show.

A small crowd hovers around the memorial along with William. I recognize two of them, Raven and Sabrina.

Jasper says a few words to William, and I watch as the man twitches and writhes, his trench coat jerking around as if he were about to haul off and deck Jasper. But he doesn't. He calms himself and nods, and soon Jasper and Leo are escorting William Helsing right off the property.

Sherlock whimpers as he looks my way. *Is that it, Bizzy? It's all over?*

I nod. "I think so."

Sprinkles bounces in my direction, and with those pink wings on her back, it looks as if she's about to lift off the ground.

Dr. Feel Good did it? She gives a sharp bark. ***I knew he was no good for my Blair. If only she would have listened.***

"Let's see what these girls have to say about it," I whisper as we head for the memorial.

It's dark out this way, save for the glow from the twinkle lights behind us.

Raven spots me and heads in my direction. "Did you see that?" She's dressed in a nurse's uniform, with the requisite short white dress and red satin gloves that ride all the way to her elbows.

I nod. "It looks as if justice is about to be served."

"I'll say. And to think, he was right in front of our faces all along." She rubs her arms in an attempt to warm herself, and my eye snags on a silver ring with a golden rose and a gem tucked in the center of it.

"That ring," I say, mostly to myself. "It's—it's so beautiful." And it's exactly like the ring Blair had on her finger—and the one stuck on the button of her blouse when she was killed. "Where did you get it?"

A devilish grin twitches on her lips. "The Midnight Maidens happen to have an entire cache of them. You'll get one tonight upon initiation. Blair hit some outlet mall last winter and bought out the supply. She really liked them. She said the rose had meaning."

I bet it did. She was dating a professor who taught at a school who has a rose as their symbol. It represented a lot more than the Maidens.

The stone glistens, and it looks to be a deep amber.

"Raven, are all the stones in the center of the rose the same color?" The one on Blair's finger was red, and the one embedded in her blouse was blue.

"Oh no, they're all different. But only a couple are coveted. One of which goes to the queen, and the other goes to the next in line." *Blair loved her boundaries when it came to the Maidens. Too bad she didn't respect boundaries in her everyday life—not even where her friends were concerned.*

"Who was the next in line to be the queen?" I hold my breath as I wait for an answer.

"It's supposed to be top secret for new members." She gives a little shrug before taking off. "But you'll know soon enough. I'd better go grab something to eat before the meeting tonight. I can't wait to give you a ring." She takes off, and I watch her as she strides back toward the fairgrounds.

Sabrina walks over with a skeleton bodysuit on, and her cartoon bones glow an eerie blue in the darkness.

"I guess it's over." She takes a quivering breath. "I knew it was him all along. He's been obsessed with Blair for the last six months. I tried to tell her it wasn't healthy." She gives Fish a quick pat between the ears.

"I guess it *is* over. And I'm glad about it, too," I say. "Poor Blair deserved justice."

Bizzy—Fish mewls—*this woman doesn't look healthy. She's all bones.*

Sherlock barks. *She looks delicious!*

Sprinkles brays out what sounds like a laugh. *Blair always did whisper in my ear that I was free to bite this woman.*

Bite Sabrina?

"Sabrina." I lean in. "Did you know William very well?"

She inches back. "Gosh, not really. I mean, other than the fact he was Dr. Feel Good." She rolls her eyes. *I hope prison feels good for him.* "Anyway, he caused a lot of pain, so I don't want to think about him."

"I get it." I glance down to her fingers and spot the silver ring with a rose. It's so dark I can't see the color of the stone, but then she moves and the moonlight shines down over it like a spotlight enlivening what looks to be a bright red droplet of blood. "I guess I'll see you later tonight, right out here."

"That's right." A smile enlivens on her lips. "It's turning out to be a wonderful, wonderful night. With William getting what he deserves, it feels as if the rest of us can finally get some closure. And a fresh start with all new Maidens, too."

And it will be my last hurrah with that money-grabbing group, but there's no need to announce it. I think we all know deep down inside this nonsense would disband without our fearless flighty leader. It takes a thief and a con man to run this kind of an operation, and Blair was both—right up until the thief ran into a killer.

Her lips curl with a mournful smile. "I've got a treat for you and your friends tonight." She pinches her ring with her thumb. "Don't worry. You're going to love it. Once you're indoctrinated into the Midnight Maidens, you'll be a Maiden for life." *And it will provide a lifetime of embarrassment to go along with it. But that's Blair's fault. Everything that's transpired these last few months has been that wicked witch's fault. I hope she's roasting in flames.*

Sabrina stalks off, and I gasp at her horrifically cruel thoughts.

"Sadly, she's not the first person to have dark thoughts about the deceased," I whisper to Fish while Sherlock and Sprinkles run around the fenced enclosure as if it were a game.

Fish let's a sharp meow rip. *I don't care for people who have dark thoughts, Bizzy. I think you should stay away from this entire Midnight Murderers organization before they murder you.*

I make a face. "You are wise beyond your years, Fish. And I promise, after tonight, I'm never going back."

"What's this?" a voice trills from behind, and I turn to see Tabitha dressed in a thick purple brocade dress, a wreath of daisies in her hair, and in her hand she holds a tambourine. "You're not talking about leaving the Midnight Maidens before you ever get initiated, are you?" She has her glasses on, and there's a sweetness to her face that makes her look vulnerable.

"Oh no," I say, holding my breath a moment because now I'm forced to lie. "I was talking about that new place over in Whaler's Cove, the Spicy Italian. I knew that meatball sandwich was trouble after just one bite, but it was so delicious I just had to keep eating it." Sort of like this lie. "Anyway, I'm fine now. And I'm really looking forward to the Midnight Maidens' initiation tonight. I've already got my money, and I know for a fact the others do, too. We're anxious to invest in our future."

"That's great." ***Thank my lucky stars. I need this. I think we all need this after Blair. And the fact she's so enthused lets me know she'll have no problem bringing in two more. I'll be queen in no time.***

Queen...

"You look adorable." I motion to her pretty costume as the moon lights up the silver threading in the brocade fabric, and she shines like an amethysts in the night.

"Thanks." She slaps her thigh. "It's my Renaissance Fair outfit. I'm a huge lover of the Renaissance Fair, so this is more of a way of life than a costume." She gives a light laugh.

My lips part. "Tabitha, can I ask who the queen will be tonight?"

"That's actually a surprise. It's color-coded according to the rings we have." She flashes a silver ring with a golden rose and a tiny purple stone, then retracts her hand just as quickly. "Oops! I wasn't supposed to say that. The rings are sort of a surprise. I'm sorry."

"Don't apologize. In fact, Raven already told me about them. I'm looking forward to getting mine."

"Oh good!" *What a relief. For once Raven blew it first.* "New girls get a green stone. It's super pretty. And they say we're only supposed to wear it to official meetings, but I've worn mine out before. It's a shame not to."

"I agree. And I won't tell," I say as we share a little laugh. "Did you hear? They've taken William Helsing in for Blair's murder." For questioning, but a part of me doesn't think that's relevant to mention. I'm hoping Jasper has already winnowed a confession out of him.

She takes in a never-ending breath. "Wow. I did not know that. I wonder if Sabrina knows?" She glances back.

Fish perks up. *Why does she care so much about Sabrina? Why not ask about Raven?*

Exactly.

I lean in. "Why would Sabrina care?"

Tabitha blinks back. "Oh, they dated. They were hot and heavy long before Blair stepped into the picture. In fact, Sabrina met him because she used to work in the administration building at that college he works at. She was there for years, and then one day out of the blue Dr. Feel Good dumped her and she lost her job. I'm guessing one had a lot to do with the other." She wrinkles her nose. "Not everyone knows that. Sabrina was pretty embarrassed about it."

My heart thumps wildly. "How did Sabrina feel about Blair and Dr. Feel Good getting together?"

Tabitha cringes. "She said she was over him and wiped her hands of the entire situation. She said she felt bad about the whole wife thing anyway." She shakes her head. "A part of me thinks that was a lot of bravado, though. Although, Sabrina did move on eventually. She got that new position at the Snake Pit, and she's doing pretty well for herself with the face painting and body art. Things were really tough for her afterwards, though—especially these last few months. She lost her condo, too, and had to move back in with her mother. That was tough because Sabrina's mother is pretty demoralizing to her. She calls her all sorts of names and badmouths her every chance she gets. It's enough to make a person lose their mind."

"Is she back on her feet yet?"

She tips her head to the woods. "I think so. She mentioned something about taking a vacation to Atlantic City soon. So that's got to be a good sign, right?"

"Right."

Fish yowls hard. *I smell a rat.*

I take a quick breath as I force a smile. "I'll see you in just a couple of hours, Tabitha."

"I'll be there with bells on." She gives her tambourine a rattle before stepping toward the makeshift memorial.

"Tabitha?" I call out her name and she turns around. "I guess I should know what I'm shooting for. What color gemstone does the queen get?"

"Red," she says brightly before dissolving into the night.

Red.

I know exactly who will be queen tonight, and suddenly all of the pieces to this murderous puzzle are falling into place.

I'm not so sure Jasper has apprehended Blair Bates' killer.

But I have a feeling he's apprehended exactly who Blair Bates' killer framed for the crime.

17

Every move she made was so well-thought-out. And yet every move was the wrong one, because ultimately, if I'm right, she'll pay dearly for her grave error.

Despite my efforts, I couldn't find my one and only suspect after I left Tabitha. So I went ahead and secured the cash for Georgie, Juni, and myself from the ground safe at the inn and headed to the woods behind the meadow at eleven o'clock just the way I was instructed.

The meadow is dark and icy at this distal end of the property. The din of music, of the overall revelry from the frightmare is slowly muted the deeper I head in that direction, and the moon up above washes the ground an ethereal shade of blue. It's wall-to-wall people here tonight, and each and every person is dressed to impress—or more to the point, *distress*.

Camila is the first person I see, with her vampy witch's dress and equally vampy face. She's a stunner in that little black dress, and I have a feeling she knows it.

"Bizzy," she hisses as she comes my way.

Fish peers out of the basket and groans. *Here comes trouble.*

Sherlock barks at the sight of her. *And she's a witch! I knew it! I knew it all along! Camila is a witch, Bizzy. Let me at her. I'll bite her ankles until she hops back on her broom and flies for the moon.*

"Sherlock." I shake my head at him. Camila needs to stay calm so nobody bolts from this little *mug* and greet.

Sprinkles whimpers. *I think we should all run for the hills before she casts a spell on us.*

Camila growls at the trio of furry creatures. "Oh hush, all of you." She snarls my way. "I've got my cash. Now what?"

"Camila, I think I know who did this."

She clucks her tongue. "So do I, you dodo. Raven called and told me they arrested Billy the Kid, right here at the spot he slaughtered Blair. Which is exactly why I think we should walk away from this financial farce."

I take a breath as a handful of girls in every type of costume enter the woods behind us. It's clear there will be more than just a few of us here tonight.

235

"I think we should go through with it," I whisper. "I have a feeling we're going to put the Midnight Maidens out of business for good."

A trio of women head this way wearing long, dark velvet, hooded cloaks, their faces lost in darkness. One of them stops off at the makeshift memorial, as the other two pull back their cloaks to reveal Raven and Tabitha.

"Five minutes," Raven calls out as she gives a friendly wave. "And your lives are going to change forever."

Camila pulls her shoulders back. "We'll be right there." She waits until they leave to pull me close by the arm. "And you'd better be there for me when I come looking to collect my five grand back at the end of the night. I'm not a wealthy woman, you know. I need that to pay my rent. And so help me, if I lose my home, I'm going to get a free room right here at the Country Cottage Inn. How would you like that?"

"I wouldn't," I snip. "And neither of us has to worry about it, because it's not going to happen."

A jumble of voices explodes from behind, and we turn to see both Georgie and Juni dancing this way.

Juni trots over dressed as a naughty schoolgirl, complete with a tiny plaid skirt that could work as a belt, a white blouse tied off under her boobs, and white knee socks with bows at the top. She's paired the look with the requisite high-heeled Mary Janes and her hair in pigtails. It's clear she's committed to the look.

"Hey, chica." Juni bumps her hip to mine. "Do you think they're going to make us take off our clothes and dance naked in a circle?"

"Not happening," Camila grunts. "Unless, of course, there's a hot man at the helm barking out orders." She shoots me a look. ***Jasper would be nice.***

I growl over at her, and she gives a wink in return.

Georgie catches up, nearly out of breath, in a bright orange kaftan with glowing purple sequins trapping the moonlight, and in her arms is that haunted doll. Annabeth looks longer, taller than I last remember. Her muslin and lace sheath appears luminescent against the shadowy night, and her pale face looks sickly. Her eyes appear to be nothing more than dark holes bored into her face, but that creepy smile never leaves her face.

"Is it time to get naked?" Georgie does an odd little hop when she says it.

"Not yet, Georgie," I whisper as I look over at the hooded woman standing alone next to the mountain of flowers set out for Blair. "We'll be there in a second. Save a place for us, would you?"

Georgie casts a sideways glance to the woods. "Okay, but we're not going in without the pooches. Come on, Sherlock and Sprinkles. You lead the way. If there's a bear in there, I want you to warn us."

Sherlock barks up at Georgie. *I don't do bears. We both know that.*

Georgie pulls out a bouquet of bacon out of her pocket. "Oh, I think you do bears, my friend," she says as if she understood him. "You do bears."

I shake my head as the four of them take off. No one understands animals quite like Georgie Conner. The bacon doesn't hurt either.

"Bear!" Juni cries as the four of them head into the woods.

Camila grunts, "If there is a bear in there, that bacon buffet she's lugging around with her will guarantee she's the first person it eats."

"If we're lucky, it'll eat the doll, too," I whisper and we share a tiny laugh. It's times like these I think that Camila could see past all the coital chaos that surrounds us. "You know you have a genuine warmth about you when you finally let down your guard."

"Then obviously I'm failing in my role as ice queen." She presses that pointed hat of hers over her head another notch as she glances to the woods. "Come on, let's get this wicked show on the road."

"In a minute," I say, looking at the hooded figure to our left and motion with my head for Camila to follow me. We make our way to the makeshift memorial, and the whites of Sabrina's eyes flash our way.

Fish gurgles. ***I don't like the look of this, Bizzy. It's too dark. All you have with you is Camila. And this woman standing in front of you looks angry enough to kill.***

Yes—she does, doesn't she?

"Hello, Sabrina," I say softly as Camila and I make our way over.

"Bizzy." The moonlight washes over her as she pulls her hood off her head. "Camila." A forced smile wobbles on her lips. "You girls ready to do what we came for?" ***As in fork over your money so I can get on with my life already.***

Fish shudders. ***She's having those dark thoughts again, isn't she, Bizzy?***

I nod.

Close enough, in my opinion.

"We're ready," I say. "This must be very hard for you." I glance to the flowers piled high on the other side of the fence. "This will all be gone tomorrow. I can see why you'd want to spend some time here."

"I can't seem to leave." She looks to the stack of hay that's still disrupted from the struggle Blair had with her killer.

Sabrina takes a step our way and her dark cloak parts, revealing those glowing bones painted onto her costume underneath.

She looks like the Grim Reaper.

She looks like death.

I can't wait for this nightmare to be over. Sabrina smirks over at the memorial. *I'm counting down the hours until they sweep away this mess. I hope they burn the hay to rubble. I don't want a trace of Blair or her blood around for another moment. Tomorrow will feel like a relief.*

"Sabrina?" I call out her name softly as Camila and I inch our way toward her. "Do you think the sheriff's department has the right person? Do you really think William was capable of doing something so heinous?"

"Oh, yes." Her eyes widen a notch. "I mean, he claimed to love her, you know. But he was married. He wasn't a good person."

"Maybe he wasn't a good person, but that doesn't mean he was a killer." The words speed out of me, and Camila shoots me a look. "Sabrina, you worked at the same school where William teaches, didn't you?"

Her mouth opens slowly. "I did." She shrugs. "I was the reason Blair met him."

I nod. "You worked at the school. In fact, you took night classes to keep busy while he was teaching his own night classes. He's the boyfriend you were telling me about, isn't he?"

She takes a quick breath. "How did you know?" She shakes her head. "I mean, it's not a secret. Of course, I took a few classes. That's how I learned my craft, remember? And Billy and I weren't serious."

My chest pumps with a dry laugh. "But you were furious when Blair stole him from you, weren't you? And she took your money, too. You lost your boyfriend, your job, and your rental because of her—all in a six-month span. You were furious with her, weren't you?"

Camilla gives me the side-eye. *You really are good.*

"Yes," Sabrina all but hisses it out, her chest pulsating violently as if she just ran a lap around all of Maine.

Fish sinks down into the basket. *Here we go.*

I take a bold step forward, and Camila stands staunchly by my side.

"You killed her, didn't you?" I whisper it low as if it were still an idea germinating in my mind.

"Yes." Sabrina closes her eyes a moment. "I killed her."

Camila gasps. "You killed Blair?" Her voice pitches a notch too loud. "How could you?"

"What do you mean, *how could I*?" Sabrina snaps back, her icy eyes trained on her old friend. "Didn't you pay attention? Oh, that's right, you're not the brightest bulb, Camila. You had the man of your dreams eating out of the palm of your hand and you had to go after another tasty treat because you're never satisfied, are you? And now look where it's got you? Teaming up with the woman that your dreamboat of an ex married. And don't you think I'm not onto this little farce you've got going on. You hired this ninny to track me down, didn't you?"

Don't listen to her. Fish growls. **You're no ninny, Bizzy.**

"I didn't know it was you," Camila shouts back defensively. "And who cares? I wasn't about to go down for something I didn't do."

"You tried to set Camila up." A tremble of a laugh comes from me as I look at Sabrina with new eyes. "You rubbed up against her when we were all looking at the crime scene. That's how Blair's blood landed on her arm, isn't it? And you were covered in body art. Nobody could tell if you were covered in blood. You came with the intent to hunt Blair down that night and kill her."

Sabrina's chest huffs. "So maybe I did? And maybe I did rub a little plasma over Camila's arm?" She looks to her old friend. "Oh, come on. You left your staff at the scene of the crime. I was in a panic. I needed to cover my tracks."

A wry smile curls on my lips. "But she wasn't the only person you were trying to set up. You did a stellar job of setting up William Helsing, too. You left those notes for me— one of which was on the school's letterhead. You broke into my home."

"Oh please, you left the door unlocked. You were practically begging for it. And yes, I wrote those notes while doing my best impression of Billy's handwriting."

"Wow," I muse. "If this went on any longer, he'd probably go to trial."

"And he will." She nods. "I'm sorry, girls, but I'm not going down for this one. We'll talk after the ceremony."

"No." It comes out flat from me. "There won't be a ceremony. I understand you're the queen tonight and looking to collect on a huge payout so you can take off to Atlantic City."

"Wow." She tosses her hands in the air. "I've only told that to one person. Obviously the wrong person." *I'm going to slaughter Tabitha next. And I won't make it quick this time. That twit has danced on my last nerve.*

"You won't be slaughtering Tabitha next," I say as I look directly into her glacial eyes. "You won't be slaughtering anyone ever again."

"That's where you're wrong." She plucks a long metal stake out of the ground and swings it wildly, striking Camila over the temple and sending her to the ground like a rag doll.

A breath gets locked in my throat as Camila lies motionless next to me.

"Camila, get up," I shout, trying to rouse her, but I can't risk taking my eyes off of Sabrina.

She takes another wild swing, and this time I catch the metal rod midair, dropping the basket with Fish in it to the ground as I do so.

Sherlock! Fish screeches so loud, her voice reverberates over the woods.

"You witch!" Sabrina spits the words into my face as we wrestle it out with that beam in her hands.

A riot of barks and growls grows louder by the second as Sherlock and Sprinkles head this way.

"Bizzy!"

I turn to see Georgie and that ghostly doll in her arms traversing their way over as well and I cringe. Georgie is the last person I'd want to endanger.

Sabrina knees me in the gut and I double over, letting out a hard *oof*.

"You don't get to ruin this for me, Bizzy." She crashes the stick over my back and sends me to the ground. "I knew you were onto me. You were relentless. And now you and your friends will have to pay." She gives a reckless swing of that stick once again toward Georgie, but thankfully, she jumps right out of the way.

Sherlock jumps up on Sabrina with such force he sends her falling backward, and I take the opportunity to leap on top of her. With one powerful maneuver, Sabrina tosses me to the side. And just as she's about to rise to her feet, Annabeth flies at her, knocking her porcelain head against

Sabrina's. Sabrina falls back to the ground with her arms spread wide, her eyes closed, and her mouth slightly ajar.

I swipe Annabeth off of her while springing to my feet.

"TKO!" Georgie shouts while pumping her fists to the sky in a victory dance. "Nice work, kiddo."

"Thank you," I say.

"I was talking to Annabeth."

Camila rouses and moans as both Sherlock and Sprinkles do their best to nudge her to wake up.

"Okay, enough." She bats them away as she struggles to sit. "Is it over?"

"It's over," I say, picking up that metal rod Sabrina was wielding and holding it like the weapon it is in the event she decides to reprise her role as the punisher. "Georgie"—I pant—"call Jasper and tell him he's got the wrong person. We've got the killer, right here."

She does just that, and the sheriff's deputies on the grounds quickly make an arrest once Sabrina comes to.

Raven and Tabitha run over with distressed looks on their faces right along with Juni and the rest of the girls.

"Juni"—I say her name sharply—"did any of the girls hand over money tonight?"

"Not yet." Her pigtails move back and forth like a couple of dried up pompoms.

"Good." I look to Raven and Tabitha. "If you drop this Midnight Maidens madness, the sheriff's department won't have anything to pursue. But believe me, if you continue to bilk anyone out of their hard-earned money, then I will sic every government agency I can after the two of you. This is poison at the bottom of the well. It's nothing but a greedy endeavor dreamed up by Blair to save her sinking financial ship. You're both better than this. Do you understand?"

The two of them offer up frantic nods.

"Bizzy," a deep voice calls out from the expanse before me, and I quickly move in that direction until I'm safe in Jasper Wilder's strong arms. "We never left Cider Cove. Leo and I ended up taking William to a coffee shop up the street in hopes he'd confess. I had a hunch I shouldn't go far." He dots a kiss to my forehead. "You did it again."

"Believe me, I would have rather you took this one to the finish line."

A sly smile rides up his cheek. "I'll take you to the finish line." He lands a searing kiss to my lips.

"That sounds like a promise I'm going to hold you to, Detective Wilder."

"It is Halloween. I've still got a couple of tricks up my sleeve."

"And lucky for me, I'm up for a treat."

He lands his lips over mine once again—and the night, all of the chaos around us dissolves to nothing.

That's the power Jasper's love has over me. He makes everything better.

Everything.

Always.

But in the back of my mind, there is one niggling thought that I wonder if Jasper and his love can ever cure— and a part of me knows he can't.

Nope. Emmie Crosby and I need to come to our own resolution, and we need to do it sooner than later or everything we've shared will be forever lost.

And that's exactly why I'm going to fix this—tonight.

18

Halloween night is still going strong.

The people attending the frightmare hardly even noticed that the sheriff's deputies hauled Sabrina Ames out of there like the killer she was. And those that did happen to notice either thought it was all a part of the show or didn't give a bat's behind.

Jasper said that William Helsing had a few interesting things to say. It turns out, William did give the money to Blair. He even cited her preference of five thousand dollar increments as per the scam she was running. William sang like a bird once he realized he might actually go up the river for a crime he didn't commit. So he told Jasper everything he wanted to know about the Midnight Maidens, which correlated with everything I had already told him.

As for Sabrina? She's pretty much toast. Not only did she confess, but Jasper mentioned forensics found her hair on Blair's bloody body—and now they know why. It's open and shut.

A part of me feels bad for Sabrina for getting tangled up in this mess. It's a hard thing when your heart gets smashed by a lousy boyfriend, even if he was already married at the time, then the girl who you thought was your best friend steals said louse of a boyfriend—and she happened to be the sole reason you're broke, too.

Camila said she's going to suggest a good legal team for Sabrina—along with a mental health defense. I guess Camila is a ride or die friend, after all.

Jasper, Leo, Camila, Georgie, Juni, and I—and, of course, our menagerie of pets, all make our way over to the Country Cottage Café. It was my decision to keep it open late tonight. I had a feeling the café would make money hand over fist on a night like tonight, and judging by the people still streaming in and out of it, I was right.

Jasper holds the door open for our motley crew, and I hang on until the last of us has gone in. Camila has snagged my attention as she slouches near the sand while scrolling through her phone.

"Why don't you go in?" I tell him as I dot a simple kiss to his lips. "I want to have a quick word with Camila." Fish squirms in my arms.

Oh, Bizzy, you're such a bleeding heart, Fish mewls. *Don't let your guard down with that one. I have a feeling she's a pro at getting hearts to bleed in an entirely different way.*

Jasper takes a breath. "Okay, I'll get you something hot to drink."

"*Ohh*, yes. Hot apple cider sounds perfect."

He hitches his head toward Camila. "She owes you one."

"Don't I know it." I give a little wink before we go our separate ways.

"Camila?" I call out over the roar of the Atlantic as the whitewash beating the shoreline holds a luminescent glow.

She turns around and frowns once she sees it's me.

Fish shudders against my chest. *Boy, is she mean. I can see why Sherlock is so grateful that you married Jasper instead of this block of ice. And if you weren't around, Sherlock wouldn't know Georgie, and he and Sprinkles wouldn't be eating bacon to their heart's content at this very moment.*

I give a slight nod, because it happens to be true.

"What it is, Bizzy?" She gives a slow blink as if she didn't have room for any more drama tonight—and believe me, I'm right there with her on that.

"I just wanted to see how you were doing. Everything okay? I mean, Blair was your friend, and Sabrina was your friend. It must be very hard."

She shrugs. "It's not easy. Blair and I weren't that close in the end, but I'll never forget her, that's for sure. And like I said earlier, I plan on being there for Sabrina." She wraps her arms around her waist as she examines me with a stern expression. "So I want to thank you for helping me. Because of you, I don't have a cloud of suspicion hovering over my head." She nods. "I knew you'd come through. Not that I don't have faith in Jasper, but he's always been so bogged down with red tape. And he insists on following all the rules. But you're a renegade, and I knew I needed someone who would buck the system and do what she wants to get the job done." Her lips pull to the side. "I'm going to say this once. I like you, Bizzy Baker—Wilder." She rolls her eyes. "And, if Jasper isn't going to spend the rest of his life with me, over some stupid mistake I apologized for a million times, well— then I'm glad he's spending it with you. I hope you give him hell." She winks along with the saucy sentiment.

A warm laugh brews in my chest. "Well, thank you. I like you, too, Camila. We've had a rocky beginning, but I'd like to think we can be genuine friends. We seem to think alike, which is a bit surprising because on the surface we seem nothing alike. But you're strong, confident, and you know what you want out of life—even if for a time that was my husband." I give a circular nod. "Anyway, I think we're past all of that. In fact, I'd like to see you find true love yourself."

Her shoulders sag with her next breath. "Yeah, well, Jasper and Leo are taken. I guess I could see where things go with Jordy again, but that never amounted to much the first time around. Maybe I'll play the singles scene for a bit and let the male pieces fall where they may. Who knows, maybe there's a future for Jordy and me, after all?"

"Maybe," I say. Jordy and Camila were loosely dating a few months back, but she's right. Nothing ever came of it.

"But, then again, your brother is a hottie." She lifts a finger in the air as if considering this.

"Yeah, but he's with Mackenzie now." I can hardly choke out those words.

"Oh dear, Bizzy." A villainous laugh ejects from her throat. "I've never let a detail like that stop me before. I'll see you later." *And that's why I'll never fully take my eyes off of Jasper.* She scowls over at Fish before taking off into the night as the darkness fully envelops her.

So much for being good friends.

Fish gasps. *She flew away on her broom, didn't she?*

"Honestly?" A laugh bucks from me. "On a night like tonight, anything is possible." We turn toward the café just as our party heads out for the tables underneath the twinkle lights.

"It's far too crowded in there," Jasper says as each one of them carries a tray full of food and quickly gets settled under the heat lamps. I swipe a sweet treat off of Jasper's tray without hesitation. My bestie may not be speaking to me, but that won't stop me from noshing on one of her jack-o'-lantern hand pies.

Sherlock barks. *Hey, Fish? Let's show Sprinkles how fast we can run from one end of the cove to the other!*

Without so much as a single mewl, Fish uses my body as a springboard and they're off to the races.

"Waitress!" Georgie calls out as she struggles to get comfortable in her seat. "I need a highchair for this little cutie."

"I'll take care of it," I say. "In fact, give me Annabeth so you can get started on your food before it turns to ice. And make sure you're right under the heater. It's freezing out here."

Georgie tosses me the doll and gets right to that big plate of pancakes in front of her.

Juni sits across from her with an identical meal at the ready.

"Hey?" Juni barks. "No fair, Mama, you didn't say mark, set, go. How am I supposed to win the battle of the pancake if you keep cheating?"

Georgie pauses with her fork in the air. "All is fair in love and pancakes."

I giggle as I turn toward the entry to the café, and all laughter in me ceases once I spot Leo holding Emmie and whispering something into her ear.

Jasper wraps his arms around me from behind. "It looks like Emmie and Leo are back on track. You ready to get there, too?"

"Oh yes," I say. "Hold onto this hand pie for me, would you?" I land the tasty treat back where I found it and head toward my bestie without hesitation.

I clear my throat as I come upon the two of them, and Emmie's eyes widen as she looks my way. She looks adorable dressed as Alice from *Alice in Wonderland*, complete with a billowy blonde wig. And I'm sure Emmie can commiserate with the characters, because she just so happens to feel as if she fell down a rabbit hole, too.

"Come here, you freak." Emmie pulls me into a tight embrace, and I can feel her chest bucking with emotion despite the fact we've pinned Annabeth between us. And soon the waterworks start, especially on my end.

Leo blows out a breath. "All right, ladies. I'm going to let you duke it out." He offers a playful short-lived smile before stepping over to Jasper in the dining area.

"How about a quick walk?" I nod toward the beach, and soon Emmie and I are on the sand. "Did you really call me a freak?" A laugh trembles from me as we stop just out of earshot of those nearby.

"Only because I love you." She shrugs. "I'm your sister, remember? I get a name-calling pass."

"Does that mean I get a horrible secret pass?"

Emmie dips her chin until her gaze is firmly pressed to mine. "Bizzy Baker Wilder, you can have any pass you want. Except, of course, anything that has to do with Leo. That boy is mine, through and through."

We share a warm laugh, but her expression grows serious once again.

"So?" She cranes her neck as she inspects me. "You've really been able to read my mind ever since Mackenzie dunked you into that whiskey barrel?"

I give a slow nod.

"*Bizzy*"—she shakes her head—"that was a million years ago. This must have been weighing on you so heavily. How could you ever think I'd cut and run? You're my ride or die. I couldn't leave your side for anything. And I do mean anything."

I press my lips tightly. I had just marveled at Camila for sticking it out with Sabrina and using the exact same phrase. And here my best friend in the world is that great and so much better.

"Oh, Em." I pull her in for another tight embrace. "I'm so sorry. Please forgive me. You should have been the first person I told."

"You're totally forgiven." She pulls back and wipes the tears from my face. "So who was the first person you shared this with?"

I make a face. "Georgie sort of wrangled it out of me."

She laughs. "That sounds about right." She takes a breath. "Leo gave me a little more detail about how you and he figured things out. And he mentioned the fact that Camila knows."

"She does know about him. Although, I've yet to verbally admit anything to her. It's sort of an unspoken truth that I share his quirk."

"Hey, don't you berate yourself. This is no quirk. You've got a bona fide superpower. And I happen to think it's pretty cool." She shrugs. "I don't mind you peeking into my head one bit."

I bite down on my lip as I nod. "Thank you, Emmie." I rattle the doll in my arms her way. "Annabeth thanks you, too."

A couple strides our way and as they step in close, we see it's my brother and the woman who landed me in this mess to begin with, Mackenzie.

"Hey, Hux." I flex a wry smile. "Mayor Woods."

"*Geez.*" Huxley shakes his head as he pulls me in for a quick hug. "Jasper just told us the news. You got another one." He steps back and examines me with his stony blue eyes. ***I will never be able to keep her safe. Good thing she married a man who's required to carry a gun.***

Mackenzie snarls my way. "Good work, I guess. But in the future, leave the detective work to the detective."

No sooner do those words leave her mouth than my very favorite detective wraps his arms around my waist from behind.

Leo joins us, as do Georgie and Juni.

Georgie pats her belly. "Great news, kiddo"—she says, looking in my direction—"I won the pancake war."

"I'm guessing you're talking to Annabeth."

Mackenzie scoffs at Georgie. "Before I leave you to carry on a conversation with your doll, I wanted to let you know that the town council has approved a Founder's Day Festival for November, which will kick off at the beginning of the month and end with a parade right down Main Street on Thanksgiving Day. Cider Cove is turning one hundred next month, and we're going to make a big to-do about it. Sure, we're practically a baby when compared to an old town like Biddeford, but Cider Cove is comprised of proud citizens and we're going to do right by this town. And we'll be highlighting all of the local businesses to the tourists who come in for the event. Expect an influx."

"That sounds great," I say as I hike up the doll in my arm a notch. "Annabeth approves, too."

Mackenzie freezes. "No haunted dolls. It's bad enough I'll have to burn an entire sage bush just to be rid of the darkness those things have tainted this town with."

"Fine," Georgie says. "But I'm really digging those quilts. Now that winter is about to ruin my sea glass hunting mojo, I think I'll take up quilting to pass the time. In fact, I'll whip up a few to sell next month for the Founder's Day Festival."

My guess is that quilts aren't all that easy to whip up, but I'll let Georgie have the fun of trying, rather than raining on her quilted parade.

Mack and Huxley take off, and Leo nods my way as he wraps his arms around his girl.

"Everything okay?"

Emmie nods while she looks my way. "Everything is great."

"It's perfect," I say just as Fish, Sherlock, and Sprinkles run up, winded from their maddening sprints. "The only thing left to do is find a home for this sweet little girl."

Georgie coos, "You mean Annabeth?"

"I mean Sprinkles," I'm quick to correct her. "That little princess deserves the best of the best."

Juni scoops the tiny treat up and kisses her on the furry forehead. Sprinkles still has her wings on from earlier tonight, albeit they're a little crooked from all the excitement.

"I think I can give her the best of the best," Juni says, looking at the tiny Yorkie. "What do you think, kid? You want to do this thing called life with me? I promise to give you lots of cuddles, kisses, and bacon. Do we got a deal?"

Sprinkles lets out a jovial bark. ***We've got a deal, Juni!*** She barks down at Sherlock and Fish. ***Hear that? I've got my forever home! And she she's going to give me bacon!*** She yips out another series of happy barks, and we all share a warm laugh.

"I think she's thrilled," I tell Juni as I give Sprinkles a stroke along her back. "In fact, I know she is. Welcome to the family, Sprinkles. You're going to be seeing a lot of us from here on out."

"All right, kid." Georgie slings an arm around Juni's shoulder. "I knew you'd give me a grandbaby one day. And now that the day is here, let's go get her settled in. But let's get one thing straight. I'm the one that gets to spoil her with bacon."

"No way, Mama. I'm spoiling this one."

"You can't do that," Georgie protests. "I spoiled you, and now look at the mess we're in?"

They take off, arguing down the cobbled path until the night swallows them whole.

"Oh no," I say, looking down at Annabeth. "Georgie forgot about this girl. Sorry, Annabeth, it looks as if you were traded in for a dog."

Emmie shrugs. "Such is the life of a doll. Maybe you and Jasper can adopt her?" she teases. "Leo and I will be the uncle and aunt who refuse to babysit."

"Very funny," Jasper muses. "I think we should put her back in her glass house and not throw any stones at it. We don't want her getting out again."

I nod up at him. "Good thinking. We should probably chain her inside just to be sure she doesn't escape. I don't think I'd make a very good parent to a haunted doll."

Leo ticks his head to the side. "You don't really think she's haunted, do you?"

"No way." I hold Annabeth out and take a look at her eerie grimace, those vacant wide eyes. "She's nothing but a clump of glorified porcelain." No sooner do the words leave my mouth than a flicker of lightning illuminates the sky as if it were noon, followed by a peal of thunder that shakes the ground beneath us. I jump so high and fast, I nearly drop Annabeth in the process.

"*Ma-ma,*" Annabeth bleats as she gives a wide-eyed blink my way, and both Emmie and I let out a shriek of terror.

Leo laughs, but Jasper remains stoic.

"What's the matter, Jasper?" Leo nods his way. "Talking doll got you a little freaked out?"

Jasper shakes his head. "More than a little. I talked to the guy from Madame Tarantula's the day I found Annabeth with that threatening note on her, and he said Annabeth was thought to be one of the most haunted artifacts in all of North America. And then he reassured me she wasn't all that menacing, because Annabeth doesn't have a talking mechanism like the other dolls do."

A muffled giggle comes from the porcelain girl in my arms and I drill out another scream.

Another flash of lightning lights up the sky once again, followed by an angry bark of thunder. Then, as if it were a reflex, I launch Annabeth skyward and she lingers overhead far longer than the laws of physics should ever allow. Her skin glows an eerie green hue as she cries out *Ma-ma* one more time.

And it's a fitting end to a very haunted Halloween.

Recipe

Country Cottage Café
Jack-o-lantern Hand Pies

Bizzy Baker Wilder here! I hope you're enjoying a wonderful autumn. It's October here in Cider Cove and the Country Cottage Café is serving the most delectable dessert. If you want a surefire Halloween treat on your hands nothing tastes better than these pumpkin hand pies. The best part? They look exactly like miniature jack-o-lanterns. They are both adorable and delicious! Happy baking!

Ingredients

Filling:

1 can pumpkin

⅔ cup evaporated milk

⅓ cup sugar

¼ cup flour

1 tsp cinnamon

½ tsp nutmeg

½ tsp ginger

½ tsp ground cloves

Crust:

2 ½ cups flour

1 stick cold butter cubed

½ tsp salt

1/3 to 2/3 cup ice water

Directions

Preheat oven to 350° (grease 9x13 pan with butter)

Filling

In a mixing bowl combine pumpkin, evaporated milk, sugar, flour, cinnamon, nutmeg, ginger, and ground cloves.

Crust

Blend butter, flour, and salt in a mixing bowl. Combine with a fork or pastry cutter until crumbly.

Slowly add 1/3 cup cold water, kneading as you go. If needed, add a bit more water.

Place in the refrigerate for 30 minutes.

Once the 30 minutes are up, roll out the dough about 1/8 of an inch thick. Use either a pumpkin-shaped cookie cutter or a sharp knife to cut out an even number of pumpkins about six inches wide.

Spray a baking sheet with nonstick cooking spray and lay the bottom of the pumpkins out flat. On the other half of the pumpkin shapes cut out Jack-o-lantern faces with a sharp knife. Feel free to get creative and have some fun!

Dollop 2 tablespoons of pumpkin mixture to each bottom half of the pumpkin. Seal with the top of your jack-o-lantern. Secure edges with a fork to seal it up.

Bake for 20 minutes, or until golden brown.

Enjoy!

A Note from the Authors

Look for **A Frightening Fangs-giving (Country Cottage Mysteries 11)** coming up next!

Thank you for reading **Butchered After Bark (Country Cottage Mysteries 10).**

Acknowledgements

Thank YOU, the reader, for joining us on this adventure to Cider Cove. We hope you're enjoying the Country Cottage Mysteries as much as we are. Don't miss **A Frightening Fangs-giving (Country Cottage Mysteries 11)** coming up next. It's Thanksgiving in Cider Cover and things are about to get spooky! Thank you so much from the bottom of our hearts for taking this journey with us. We cannot wait to take you back to Cider Cove!

Special thank you to the following people for taking care of this book—Kaila Eileen Turingan-Ramos, Jodie Tarleton, Margaret Lapointe, and Lisa Markson. And a very big shout out to Lou Harper of Cover Affairs for designing the world's best covers.

A heartfelt thank you to Paige Maroney Smith for being so amazing in every single way.

And last, but never least, thank you to Him who sits on the throne. Worthy is the Lamb! Glory and honor and power are yours. We owe you everything.

About the Author

Bellamy Bloom

Bellamy Bloom is a **USA TODAY** bestselling author who writes cozy mysteries filled with humor, intrigue and a touch of the supernatural. When she's not writing up a murderous storm she's snuggled by the fire with her two precious pooches, chewing down her to-be-read pile and drinking copious amounts of coffee.

Visit her at:

www.authorbellamybloom.com

Addison Moore

Addison Moore is a **New York Times**, **USA Today** and **Wall Street Journal** bestselling author who writes mystery, psychological thrillers and romance. Her work has been featured in *Cosmopolitan* Magazine. Previously she worked as a therapist on a locked psychiatric unit for nearly a decade. She resides on the West Coast with her husband, four wonderful children, and two dogs where eats too much chocolate and stays up way too late. When she's not writing, she's reading. Addison's Celestra Series has been optioned for film by **20th Century Fox.**

Feel free to visit her at:

www.addisonmoore.com

Made in the USA
Las Vegas, NV
15 October 2022

57358543R00148